CW00857328

THE SYSTEM

PROTECT A CHILD?

Katharyn Dunn

WESTBOW
P R E S S®
A DIVISION OF THOMAS NELSON
& ZONDERVAN

This is a work of fiction. All of the characters, names, incidents, organizations, and dialogue in this novel are either the products of the author's imagination or are used fictitiously.

WestBow Press books may be ordered through booksellers or by contacting:

WestBow Press
A Division of Thomas Nelson & Zondervan
1663 Liberty Drive
Bloomington, IN 47403
www.westbowpress.com
1 (866) 928-1240

Scripture taken from the King James Version of the Bible.

ISBN: 978-1-9736-8840-2 (sc)
ISBN: 978-1-9736-8839-6 (hc)
ISBN: 978-1-9736-8841-9 (e)

Library of Congress Control Number: 2020904872

Print information available on the last page.

WestBow Press rev. date: 05/07/2020

INTRODUCTION

Robin McDaniel was startled from her sleep when the phone rang. She looked at the clock; it was three o'clock in the morning. Her stomach ached at the realization that this was yet again a call from one she had come to believe was kin to the evilest people alive. "Hello," she said, trying her best to hide any sign of fear in her voice. They were relentless, calling all hours of the night to disrupt her sleep.

There was a moment of silence on the other end of the line. "Don't sleep too sound tonight. I'd hate for you to wake up too late to get out while your house is burning." This was followed by his evil laughter, which sent chills down Robin's spine as she hung up the phone. She always answered; she had to. Her son was working night shifts at the ER, and she had her precious grandbabies in her care. What if it was Sampson and something was wrong? Or if he just needed the reassurance from his mother that she and his two young daughters were all right. Fools, didn't they know she never slept soundly. She never could prove who the calls came from since they were made from various payphones around Maverick, but she knew.

Zorro, the large gray wolf and shepherd mix, sat silently staring out the window as a truck slowly passed by on the lime rock road. A low hum grumbled deep in his chest. "Just another night on guard, Zorro. Good boy. Go check the perimeter." Robin opened the door and the dog silently made his way out to patrol the yard. She walked back to her room and knelt at the end of her bed, hands folded, and head placed atop them, she prayed aloud, "Lord, I need your help. I need the strength to endure this tribulation and the fortitude to protect my son and granddaughters, Amen." With a deep sigh, which slightly lightened the tension in her shoulders, she crawled back into her bed and fell asleep, but she tossed and turned the rest of the night.

Sampson arrived home at seven in the morning, just in time to relieve his mother for her day at work at the same hospital. "Good morning, Mama," he said. The dark circles under her eyes answered the question he didn't need to ask; they hadn't stopped calling. "I'm sorry, Mama. I love you."

"I love you too, honey. Take care of the babies. I'll be back in time for dinner, before you have to leave." Robin grabbed her purse and headed out the door, calling Zorro back into the house. She knew that after breakfast with the babies, Sampson would crash, and Zorro would be able to wake him if something went amiss.

Robin, her two teenage sons, Sampson and Mark, two horses, Sterling and Blaze, Zorro, and a white barn cat named Jose moved to a small, sleepy, rural town in north-central Florida called Maverick. Robin was a pretty woman with ash-blonde hair and big brown eyes. She was average height and weight and kept in good physical shape with exercise and playing with the boys and the animals. She worked as an RN. She and her family moved to the area to attain her master's degree in the medical field. She was a gentle, nurturing soul with the quick, intelligent mind of a lifelong learner. As a single mother, attaining an advanced degree would increase her ability to support her family. Robin and her sons joined a local church, where she became active in the women's Bible study group and sang in the choir. Besides being a full–time college student, she worked part-time in a nearby hospital.

Not thrilled about the move so far from home, Sampson decided to explore the rural, one-horse town that he found himself in. It didn't take long to see everything the town of Maverick had to offer. With a predominantly white population, and over half of the four thousand inhabitants under the age of twenty, not many people were seen on the streets. As Sampson drove through the town's only flashing traffic light, he observed a hardware store on one corner, a bar on the opposite corner, and a convenience store on another. The typical lunch crowd was gathered at the Country Time Buffet and the same for Gilly's BBQ Joint. The local grocery store parking lot was also fairly busy, full of women collecting food that was not grown in their own backyards. On initial observation, women seemed to still play the traditional role of homemaker, which made Sampson chuckle. His mama was definitely not from around here. The one gas station, the Seed and Feed farm store, and one beauty salon and barbershop combo were heavily outnumbered by the six churches of different denominations. According to what his mother had said, the elementary school was shared by Maverick's youth and those of the neighboring town. The high school Sampson was to attend was quite small compared to where he came from. Grades 10, 11, and 12 had a total of about six hundred students. In the center of town was the county courthouse and a small post office.

It didn't take long to drive out of town, where fields or pine tree–covered areas took over. In the middle of an open hayfield was a single-wide mobile home. Since an ambulance and fire truck were parked under a tin carport out front, Sampson assumed it was used as the fire and EMS station.

This was a farming community, which was reflected by the attitudes and personalities of its inhabitants. Rough around the edges, the land and farmers smelled like a combination of fertilizer and farm animals, hay, high-grade tobacco, and sweat. Cows grazed in the fields alongside goats and horses. Hogs and beef were raised at home for food and were often hauled off for processing at the local butcher.

Sampson laughed at the chickens running down the side of the lime-rock road as he questioned if one would choose to cross it. He followed an open-sided stock trailer, common to see. It must have just dropped a load of cattle off to the butcher because fresh manure was falling off the back of the trailer in front of him with each bump in the road. The typical cow pony was tied inside the trailer, fully tacked. Interestingly enough, when the horses became too old to work, they could very well take their last ride in that trailer to be slaughtered and made into dog food. Such was the cycle of life in Maverick. If you were anybody around here, you had to have livestock, land, a big truck, a cow pony or two, and a stock trailer. As Sampson drove around the area, he reflected about how different his new life would be now that his parents separated and his Mom and brother moved to Maverick.

Sampson McDaniel-Perez was an extremely handsome and popular young man. He had dark, wavy, thick hair, golden-brown eyes, and a stunning smile after enduring a few years with braces. He stood six foot three inches. Some people said he had a striking resemblance to Elvis with a cool, laid-back personality to match. His friends and family called him "Little Sam" because his father, although a head shorter, was called "Big Sam."

Though unhappy about the move at first, things went better than Sam might have expected. School came easily for Sam; he was an honor-roll student as well as a jock. Football and baseball were highlights of Sam's years at Maverick High School, but what he really looked forward to was working with animals. Future Farmers of America (FFA), allowed Sam to do just that at school, and 4-H provided the same opportunity outside school. He showed a quarter horse in the American Quarter Horse Association; AQHA, and in 4-H, he served as judge for the youth 4-H classes and was exceptional at working with the four to twelve-year-old youth. Sam was also on the national 4-H horse judging team. He and his beautiful bay gelding, Sterling, were a winning team who went to nationals every year. Sam was active in the local Baptist church, participating in many youth activities and Bible study groups. He accepted Jesus as his personal savior at an early age, while attending day care during school vacations. He was baptized and dedicated into God's family as an infant.

Sam's nature, according to his mom, could be

summed up as "Teen Mister Wonderful," though Robin might have been a little prejudiced. He was always respectful, empathetic, and loved to laugh and joke around. Sam's childhood showed him how to love others and be thankful to God. He was champion of the underdog, a great white knight who could fix the world's problems with his gallant steed, sword, and shield. Because of his work in 4-H and good grades, Sam was a candidate for a full scholarship at the University of Florida's Agricultural College and on his way to make something of himself at a young age. Then he met Jill.

Sam was in his element. It was the end of spring, which meant two things. Baseball would be wrapping up soon, and the big 4-H and state fair agriculture shows were just around the corner. He was more than ready! He and his beautiful bay quarter horse had quite a handle on taking blue ribbons from almost every arena they entered together. Sterling's coat was a shiny golden-brown. He had a black mane and tail, two white stockings on his back legs, and a wide white blaze running down his face. "Good morning, Sterling," Sam said to his horse as he ran his hands gently down the sides of the gelding's muzzle. Sterling knew the drill. It would begin with a big scoop of sweet-feed grain paired with a nice grooming. Sterling nudged his head against Sampson's back as he turned to walk out of the stall, pushing him forward as if to say, "Hurry up and get my food!" Sampson laughed and quickly returned with Sterling's breakfast. They were quite a pair; the golden-brown coat of the shining horse matched the color of Sam's eyes perfectly. With daily care, the horse's mane and tail gleamed black, which matched Sam's wavy hair. Before a show, Sam constructed an elaborate braid in the tail of his steed; the angel-cage braid was his new favorite. But it took a while, and getting faster meant a lot of practice, and the Maverick cheerleaders' long hair provided the opportunity for him to practice and flirt at the same time. "All in the name of winning at the state fair." He would say.

"Only one more week until the River County Fair, Sterling, we have to stay in shape," Sam said. Sam tossed the heavy western saddle onto his horse's back and secured the girth. As soon as Sterling tried to lick two layers of plastic from the inside of his feed bucket, Sam bridled him and led him from his stall into the fenced yard. The five-acre parcel made a perfect size track to warm up, and the large, mostly treeless yard acted as the perfect arena. Sampson ran through his routine with Sterling, cooled him off, hosed him down, and left him to graze in the yard while he went to school. When he came home from baseball practice, Sam was greeted, as usual, by Sterling's happy but hungry whinny. Sam found Sterling standing in front of his stall, impatiently looking at his feed bucket. With a laugh, Sam let him in the stall, poured him a heaping scoop of feed, and brushed him down before heading to the house for supper.

When the day of the first big show finally arrived, Sam was excited, and Sterling reflected his giddiness. "Calm down boy." Sam coaxed the jittery gelding to relax with a handful of baby carrots. After they were settled in their temporary home base, Sam left Sterling to chew on his flake of alfalfa hay and went to explore the grounds. "I'm going to go scope out the competition, boy. I'll be right back." With that, Sam walked off to inspect the barns and grounds. Competition was going to be tough this year. There were some magnificent horses here. *It's all about the presentation*, he reminded himself, and the gleam of confidence came back into his eyes. Not many could hold a candle to Sterling. Big Sam had made sure of that by drilling everything he needed to know into Sampson's head long before Sterling could even be ridden. Big Sam made sure his son had the best tack and western outfits that money could buy. He provided a new matching truck and a red two-horse trailer to transport them in classic style.

There were countless animals and people to see at the fairground, and Sam enjoyed every minute of it. Being only Thursday, many more would arrive before the shows began on Friday. He wandered through the aisles that housed rabbits, chickens, goats, sheep, pigs, and cows. He was always fascinated by how well these animals did in the show ring. None of them seemed as smart as his horse, but they all managed to do exactly as they were supposed to. He respected the work that must have gone into their preparation. And then there was the fact that they were sold there; all that work went into someone's freezer. He definitely preferred taking his steed home.

Sam was making his way through the cattle when he spotted a girl who captured his full attention. She wasn't a supermodel, but something about her stopped him dead in his tracks. Her eyes. She had a look of challenge and a confident air. Her slender body and slight curves were met with long legs covered by dark blue denim that ended at dusty brown boots. He watched her unload bales of hay for her steer to bed in and eat, as well as a bucket of feed. He walked closer and continued to watch as she began working with her steer. Her short brown hair was pulled back from her face in a small ponytail, and her large brown eyes softened as she spoke to the animal. *Okay,* he thought, *I have to talk to this girl.* "Seems like a ton of work for a steak," Sam said lightly, which got her attention immediately.

"He's worth a lot more than just a steak, sir." Jill snapped.

"Oh, I'm sure he is. I like hamburgers too. And roast beef." The girl just looked at him and remained silent. "I'm just joking. I didn't mean to offend you. That's a nice cow."

"He's a steer; cows are females," she said with a hint of amusement pulling at the corners of her full lips and her eyes smiling.

"Thanks for the lesson. I'm mostly a horse person. My name is Sampson, but my friends call me Sam."

"Jill," she said, extending her hand to him.

Sampson took her hand briefly and nodded once in a manner of southern politeness. "Where are you from?"

"Maverick. I'm a senior at the high school there."

"Really? You mean we go to the same school and have never met?"

"Ha! Well apparently, we do." She replied

Sampson was perplexed, but after a little digging, he figured out that their schedules kept them at opposite ends of campus at any given time during the day. "So how did you get into raising cows? I mean steers."

"My daddy taught me how to raise them from the time they are born until we show them in the arena. I have three steers—a newborn, a yearling, and a show-ready two-year-old. That way I have one ready for every year. You have to start working with him at only a few days old. Putting a halter on him is step one. Then we tie him to a post with a quick release knot, and he learns not to fight against the lead rope. Once he gets that down, I can start touching him, petting, and scratching, which they usually love. The next step is to get him to walk and stand still. Daddy started teaching me all of this when I was little, and I showed my first steer when I was eight. He's always called me his special daughter." She said.

Jill shared that she was not from a broken home but from a home that was similar to a shattered windshield. Although connected, the family could not be considered functionally normal. When Sampson asked what she meant by that, she looked away and said, "Daddy taught me how to start them leading and standing properly, how to groom them, and how to present them to the judge. This is not common for girls. He picked out all the clothes I was to wear in the ring. He and I would go shopping and then have lunch, just the two of us. It was a father and daughter thing; my Mom never got into this part of my life; she doesn't like animals much. She mainly cooks and cleans and plays with my brother. Learning all of this takes a long time, and Daddy really likes it when, after so many long hours in the barnyard, we can show and win. He really likes to win. When we win, he tells me how special I am." Jill explained.

"It's still hard for me to show at the fair, knowing that the people who bid on the steers take them away to be made into steaks and hamburger since they can't be used for breeding. They weigh every steer, and each contestant gets paid by the pound depending on the quality of the meat and their place in the show. Blue ribbon winners pay the most. This is how Daddy and I make our expenses. And I get a little of the money to buy some school clothes or something I really want. This part is hard, but I really want Daddy to be happy and proud of me." Sam noticed a fleeting, far-away look come across Jill's face. But just as quickly as it appeared, it disappeared. Sam said goodbye then as he had to go to the horse barns to check on Sterling and polish his tack for his first show the next day. "I will try to come by and watch you show your steer tomorrow," Sam said.

"That would be cool. I'd like to catch one of your

shows too. It was nice to meet you." Jill replied. She watched as he walked away with the same look on her face. She would never tell anyone what being a "special daughter" really meant.

Sam and Jill started casually dating not long after meeting. They would meet after football practice, have a cold drink, talk about the fun they had in 4-H, and what they were going to do after graduation. Sam was heading off to collage as he had been awarded a Bright Futures scholarship and a full agricultural scholarship to the University of Florida—UF. He planned to live in the freshman dormitory on campus his first year. Jill did not like school, so she guessed she would have to find a job. She really did not have many skills outside of home and 4-H. Jill thought she could work as a farmhand or as a salesperson at a store in the mall. But they still had most of their senior year ahead of them, so she did not have to make plans just yet. "You should apply to the community college and complete your basic studies," Sam encouraged. "Then you would have your associate's degree and could get a better job." Jill wrinkled her nose but said she would look into it. They still had plenty of time.

The Friday night high school football games were a major form of entertainment for the locals and highly attended. You had to get there early or take a chance of not finding a seat in the bleachers. Sam was a starting receiver on the team. He practiced every day after school.

Robin and her younger son went to every home game. They usually saw Jill, her father, Peter Stone, her young sister, Kelly, and brother, Pete Jr., sitting together in the stands. But they usually would not acknowledge her. The concession stand was staffed by parent volunteers, who cooked hamburgers, hot dogs, and fries, and served cold drinks and water. They did a booming business and donated all of the profits to the team. Jill's mother, Lisa Mae, volunteered in the kitchen and was seldom seen watching a game.

After the coach released the team at the end of each game, Jill would run out to Sampson, cling to his arm, and kiss his cheek. They were becoming very close, which made Robin very nervous about their relationship. She warned him more than once, "Sampson, you are getting ready to go off to college. Please don't get too involved with this girl," to which he replied, "Don't worry so much, Mama. I've got this." Robin sent many prayers to heaven for the well-being of her son. He was so smart and yet so naïve at the same time. "Jesus, please guide Sampson's path and direct his thoughts to glorify your name."

As a regular part of Maverick's entertainment,

Mud bogs were held regularly every other Saturday night in a large open field just out of town. Jill and Sam loved to go to the mud bogs and watch the local men and women compete for fame and fortune. To prepare the bogs, tractor-created long deep ditches were filled with water, and the soil was turned to make thick dark mud. The drivers of four-wheel drive trucks, jacked-up dune buggies, and Jeeps competed in divisions to see who could make it through the bog without getting stuck. This was a regular date for Sam and Jill since the price of admission was only five dollars. The locals held side bets, and designated "bookies" took the money and keep track of the bets. It was cheap entertainment.

On one of these dates, a man who had been drinking stumbled and poured his beer across both of Jill's feet. "Oh no," she exclaimed. "If I go home smelling like beer, Daddy will beat me!" Sampson found a water hose and had Jill take off her shoes and socks so he could spray them off. "How do I explain the drowned socks and shoes now? And they still kind of smell like beer." Jill cried. "Let's get out of here."

Sampson scooped Jill up and carried her to his little truck, her socks and shoes in her hands. "Your shoes aren't too wet. Put them in the bed of the truck. You take one sock, and I'll take the other." Jill began laughing hysterically as Sam drove off, his arm out the window and holding the wet sock. "Only thing I can think of. You do the same with the other one." They spent the rest of their time together that night driving around, airing out her socks so she would not get into trouble.

When he dropped her off at home, her socks were almost dry, and the beer smell was gone. "Thank you. You are my hero," Jill said, lovingly joking. Then she kissed Sam.

Senior year was rapidly coming to an end. It was the end of May, and spring was in full swing at Maverick High. To some seniors, it meant the end of a long hard road. To others it meant the beginning of a whole new journey. This was the way it seemed to both Jill and Sam. But before the school year came to an end, the senior prom was to be held in the school gymnasium. The gym was decorated with the school colors of blue and gold. Paper streamers and balloons were hung from the ceilings, and a stage was built for the DJ to set up his equipment. A huge banner was hung outside of the gym entrance that said, "Welcome Class of 1986."

Prom night would be a gala affair. When Jill told her parents that Sam had asked her to be his date, they were delighted until Jill told them that she would need a formal gown and matching shoes for the big dance. "We can't afford a new gown and shoes for one night of foolishness," her father exclaimed. "Call your cousin in Valdosta. They have money. See if you can borrow what you need," he added. Jill was devastated. She knew her parents did not have a lot of money, but they always made sure she had the best clothes for her 4-H shows. Why not now?

Jill called her cousin and was able to borrow a pretty gown and shoes from her. The gown was a light blue floor-length with thin straps and a pink ribbon that tied around her waist. Her shoes were satin heels dyed to match the gown. They were a half size too small, but she would not complain. "Thank you so much," Jill told her cousin. "This dress is really beautiful, and I probably would not been able to go to the prom if you did not lend it to me. I will be very careful with it," she promised.

The week before prom night, Jill became more and more nervous. She had never learned how to dance. When she asked her mother to show her, Lisa Mae just gave her strange look; she had never been on a dance floor in her life. Daddy had been acting strange lately, so Jill did not ask him if he could teach her how to dance. But Jill wanted to go to the prom with Sam, and she did look good in her beautiful gown.

Sam had the time of his life at the prom. He was

a great dancer and so handsome and popular in his tuxedo. His dance card was full with dance requests from the most popular girls in the senior and junior classes. "Well, don't be a wallflower. Dance with me, my lady," Sam said, bowing slightly, crooked arm extended toward Jill. "You look beautiful tonight," he whispered in her ear.

"I really don't know how to dance." Jill said, blushing.

"That's okay. I'll show you. I lead, you follow." Jill slid her hand around Sam's elbow, and he quickly swooped her out onto the dance floor.

Sam made her feel like a princess, a normal, loved girl with the most amazing boyfriend who would surely care for her forever. He had fallen in love with Jill, so he was cautious not to step on her feet or embarrass her as he twirled her around on the dance floor. "I've never known anyone quite like you Sampson."

"That's because I'm one in a million," Sam said and chuckled lightly.

Jill replied, "Please don't ever leave me."

"Now why would I do a thing like that?"

His half smile was enough to light up the room for Jill. She had a sense of security with Sam. He would be her provider, her savior from the world of turmoil that she came from. With the start of the next slow song she laid her head on his shoulder as he smoothly shuffled them around in a small circle.

Just before prom ended, Sam and Jill made their exit relatively unnoticed. This gave them ample time to have Jill home before curfew. Jill thought about telling Sam about her "special" relationship with Daddy but could not on this magical night. She wondered, *Would he understand the ten years of abuse? Would he blame her, or would he protect her and save her?*

After graduation, Daddy lost all interest in Jill. His attention went to his younger daughter, who was ten years old. Kelly was the middle child, a pretty, soft-spoken girl with blonde curls that hung softly around her face. She now became Daddy's new "special daughter" and finally got the attention that she thought she wanted and deserved for the past several years.

Jill was desperate. She was out of school, had no job, was too old for 4-H, and too old for Daddy. What was she to do? Her next logical step in life seemed to be get married, be a housewife, and maybe have a child of her own. There were no major ambitions for her future, which was status quo for most Maverick women. Sam was her dream come true. He would give her exactly what she wanted, what she needed.

Sam took a summer job in a grocery store, packing groceries and taking them to the customers' cars. "Is plastic okay?" he would ask with a smile. If he were really nice, he might get a tip. He wanted to save some money to help Robin with any expenses his scholarship did not cover. Jill, with nothing much to do during the day, often went to the store to talk and make out with Sam during his breaks and lunch hour.

On one of these visits, Jill decided to tell Sam all her secrets and confessed that Daddy began abusing her when she was eight. He would come into her room at night, lie next to her, and begin the progressive fondling until it became a complete sexual encounter. He would tell her how special she was and how much he loved her. "I love you more that anyone in the whole wide world, but you can't tell anyone. This is our very own secret," he would say. Jill was scared at first, but the back rubbing did feel good and the fondling began to feel normal to her. As with most victims of child abuse, Jill reacted with mixed emotions. She felt guilt, helplessness, and embarrassment. Sometimes she cried or shook. She felt anxious and confused that Daddy would come back, or might not come back. She had abrupt mood changes with thoughts of aggression and bouts of depression. But worst of all was the lack of being able to concentrate on anything unless Daddy was close by. She was totally dependent on him for his attention. But now she was too old for Daddy. She was out of school and 4-H. And was totally alone except for Sam.

"I just can't stay there any longer, Sam, and I don't have any place to go. Daddy loves Kelly now," Jill said, crying.

"Can't you go to your mother? Surely she'll do something to help you, to help Kelly."

"My mother has never been there for me or my sister. The only one she loves is my little brother. I tried telling her years ago, and she just told me I was lying and that if anything was happening, it was my fault."

"How in the world could that be your fault?" Sampson was infuriated. For the first time in his life, Sam felt hate and contempt. He had no idea how to handle the situation.

"She said that I shouldn't wear tight blue jeans or my shorts were too short. She said I was teasing him and leading him on."

"This is sick. You know that, right? Your family is horrible!"

"Can you please help me get out of there? Maybe we can get a place together. I can get a job at the store where my mother works, and then maybe we can afford something together."

"I am supposed to be leaving for college in a couple

of months. That wouldn't be a smart move because then you'd be in the place alone."

"You said you'd never leave me."

"I'm not leaving you. I'm building our future."

"But what am I supposed to do when you go off to college? Just sit here and wait for the next four years?"

"Have you thought about going to school for something? And I won't be far away. I'll come home on the weekends. Maybe Mama will let you move into our place."

Jill was right about her mother; she would not help. Lisa Mae was the third of twelve children born to parents who lived in a poor country community in the Deep South. The first two children were boys, who were expected to work the crops. The main crop was tobacco, and the work was very hard. Lisa Mae was expected to run the household and care for the remaining children. Her mother was pregnant or nursing an infant for over fifteen years and did not have time or energy to provide a nurturing environment. She taught the girls how to plant vegetables, harvest, and can them for the future needs of the family. Lisa Mae's grandmother lived with the family and did the sewing, darning socks, and quilting with the scraps she could salvage from old clothes that could not be handed down. Lisa Mae did not go to school, but she could read and write to some degree. Her grandmother sometimes told Lisa Mae and her sisters stories from the Bible that she could remember. The remaining male children worked in the tobacco fields. Lisa Mae met Jill's father, Pete Stone, and married him when she was fifteen. She left her family and never looked back.

Lisa Mae was not a pretty woman. She was never taught how to dress fashionably or style her hair, and makeup was out of the question. Years of stress and hard work, lack of education, and lack of love and nurturing made her totally subservient to her domineering husband. She was compliant, obedient, dutiful, and accommodating to him and everyone else she came in contact with.

For many years, Lisa Mae convinced her family that she had a heart problem and was taking medications for it. Very pale and extremely thin, she would hold her chest and even faint when the need arose. Whether this heart condition was true, Daddy used this information to keep Jill from telling her mother of her special status. "If your mother found out about our loving relationship, she would be jealous and could even have a heart attack and die. You don't want her to die, do you? You know you are my favorite, and I love you with all my heart," Daddy would say.

Lisa Mae ignored her daughters and spent all her attention and even love, as she knew it, on her young son, Pete Jr., who was eight years old, was small for his age and not a good student. He resembled his mother. He had the body of a runner and loved to run and jump over homemade hurdles in the yard. Lisa Mae often sat outside in a folding chair and cheered him on. Jill was right; she could never confide in her mother again as she knew, from past experience that she would not be believed.

"Mama, Jill needs to get out of her house. Can she come here and live with us? She can get a job while I go to school and help you out with housework and rent. I really love her, Mama, and want to help her out." Sam pleaded. He did not, however, tell his mother about the abuse.

Robin was blown away with Sam's request. She could easily see that Jill was manipulating her son and looking for an easy way out from the rules and restrictions of her childhood home. Robin would never allow Jill and Sam to live together under her roof. Robin prayed for the wisdom to handle this situation. She had a friend who lived several blocks away, the single mother of a young daughter. She had mentioned several times that she would like to have a live-in student to help her take care of her pets and her daughter while she was at work. This seemed like the perfect solution to both problems. A win-win, right?

This arrangement worked out well for about a month. But it was not what Jill wanted. She felt like she would lose Sam if she wasn't with him all the time. She needed Sam. He was her lifeline, and this just wasn't the security she needed.

Jill would sneak over to Sam's house when Robin was at work to spend quality time with him. Jill did not fulfill her commitment with Robin's friend. When she visited Sam, she left the child taking a nap, alone in the house. She did not clean or even do the dishes. The pets went without food and clean water. And Jill did not look for a regular job.

Robin's friend soon became frustrated with this behavior and asked her to leave. Jill went crying to Sam. "This just isn't fair. She wants me to be her slave," Jill complained.

Robin had developed a strong dislike for this girl based on the belief that she would keep Sam from making something of himself. She still would not agree to allow this manipulative girl to live in her house with her family. What initially sounded like a win-win had rapidly become a lose-lose. Jill was so angry with Robin that she wrote her a note and left it in her bedroom. It said, "I am going to get your son any way

I can, and if you don't like it, you can kiss my tail!" Robin confronted Sam with the letter and asked him if he knew about it and if he read it.

"I knew she put something in your room, but I was watching TV and did not go in there, Mama. And I did not read it," Sam said. Robin was not used to disrespect, and she was not sure if her son was being completely honest with her. She had to think; she had to pray. Should she compromise her values to accommodate this existing relationship between Jill and Sam? She was beginning to have doubts. Surely it could not be the Lord's plan to have Sam sacrifice his education, his scholarship, his promising future for the puppy love of a willful nineteen-year-old girl who was clearly only thinking about herself. Were Sampson and Jill praying?

"Will you come to church with me so that we can pray together and see what the Lord thinks we should do?" Sam asked.

Jill looked at him and replied with feigned patience, "We never really went to church, but I believe there is a higher power. I tried to talk to him once when I was little. I asked him for help, but he never helped me. He won't help me now; I have to help myself. You can go in if you want, and I will wait for you outside."

Sam went into the church, but as he knelt at the

altar, he couldn't concentrate on his prayers. "God, I am so angry right now. How could you have let these horrible things happen? What am I to do now to help Jill? Help me know what to do."

Jill soon made good on her promise to get Sam any way she could. She became pregnant. Sam was to become a father in a few short months. They were desperate to find a place to live. Knowing that they could not stay with Robin, they moved into a rundown travel trailer on her grandmother's property just outside of town. The trailer was about six feet wide by fourteen feet long. There was a small bunk bed at one end, a mini kitchen with a two-burner stove, and a combined eating area and living room. It had a combined chemical toilet and shower that sometimes had warm water. College was now out of the question for Sam. Besides his summer job packing groceries, Sam took a second job as a salesman at a local hardware store. He worked at the hardware on the day shift and at the grocery store evenings and weekends, both for minimum wage. Jill was on welfare and collecting food stamps. Sometimes Sam could bring home unsold meat or vegetables.

The couple went to Robin and asked her to finance a nice wedding for them so that the baby could have Sam's last name. With school, a younger son, and bills,

Robin could not afford to finance a wedding, so they went to his father. Big Sam and one of his hunting buddies agreed to help with a small outdoor wedding on his property near the hunting woods. The scene was rustic but beautiful as the property had a small pond and big trees. Jill wore a very pretty, borrowed, long white dress and a veil trimmed with blue ribbons. She carried a single white carnation and walked down a grass aisle, pregnant and without her family. Sam, a few guests, and the justice of the peace watched her approach. Big Sam and Robin watched from the sidelines with great sadness in their hearts. This was not the future that they had planned for their son. Sam was very handsome in a dark-blue sport jacket, white shirt, blue tie, jeans, and polished cowboy boots. But there was no look of happiness on his face. They were babies having a baby.

After the ceremony they cut a small homemade cake. Robin left the wedding and went home. This was the saddest day of her life. She got on her knees and prayed once again. "Lord, I don't understand your plan. I am so sad that my precious son has sacrificed his whole future for this girl and that he is now going to be responsible for a whole new life. Lord, open my eyes to your plan, and help me to trust you to have this under your perfect control." Robin fell asleep crying.

Big Sam and Salvage Sal had been friends and hunting buddies for many years before Sam was born. When Sam turned two years old, he had his first experience with Uncle Sal. Sam never knew Sal's real name but loved him like a real uncle. Sal would salvage anything that would bring him money. His main crop was old copper wire that could be found in bulk in the big onsite Dumpsters at construction and building demolition sites. As he grew, Sampson could remember spending many Saturday nights standing around a fifty-gallon drum burning the coating off the copper wire with his father and Uncle Sal. The wire had to be burned at night to keep the environmental police from finding out about the pollution caused by burning the rubber coating. In addition to his salvage business, Sal had a hog management business and managed hunting campsites in several of the pine tree farms in the area. The owners of the pine tree farms had thousands of pine trees growing in several stages of development, from sapling through trees ready to cut down for transport to the lumberyards. The owners also ran hunting camps and sold camping and hunting memberships to hunters and their families throughout the country. Members came during hunting season and either ran walker coonhounds or beagles to flush out the deer or boars. Some hunters preferred to put up a camouflaged blind or tree stand, and hunt with bow and arrows or shotguns and rifles. In the evenings, they gathered around the campfire and swapped stories about the trophies they had hanging in their dens or the ones that got away.

From the time he was walking, Big Sam and Uncle Sal took Sam with them to help with hog management. To manage the hog population required castrating most of the young boars and cropping one ear so that the hunters could tell the difference between the boars and the barrows. Both boars and barrows grew tusks, but boar meat was musky and rank. Since most hunters ate the meat, they preferred the better-tasting meat from the barrows. Uncle Sal flushed out the hogs by turning a pack of walker coonhounds loose in the woods. After the dogs surrounded a hog, Sal turned loose one or two pit bull catch dogs. These dogs were trained to catch and hold a hog by its ears until the castration and cropping were completed. The pit has very strong jaws, and Uncle Sal or Big Sam often had to put a leash on the dog and use a strong stick to pry them off the hog. Sam was put in a safe place, either on a tree limb or in the back of a pickup.

When dealing with a sow and her piglets, Sal put corn in a large trap that was big enough for her to get into but not big enough for her to turn around. Her piglets would stay close to their mother and could be caught, castrated, and cropped. Sam got to hold some of the squealing piglets until the job was done.

Sampson and Goodtimes

So, with years of friendship, love, and good times between them, when Sam asked Uncle Sal for help with his wedding, he agreed, saying, "I will help you out with this wedding, but I think you are making a big mistake."

Robin was on a two-week vacation when Jill went into labor. She delivered a beautiful baby girl. Jill named her Laurel, and Sam was immediately head over heels in love with his new baby daughter. He immediately called Robin and was absolutely giddy. "Mama, you have to come home and see my baby girl.

She is so beautiful, healthy, and looks just like me." Jill had a relatively easy delivery, according to the nurses, and was very hungry soon afterward. This was a good sign. Robin came home to visit her new granddaughter and totally agreed with her son that this beautiful baby was indeed a gift from God. Jill chose not to nurse her daughter so that she could sleep all night, and Sam could get up in the middle of the night and give Laurel a bottle, burp her, and change her diaper. He did this happily and without complaint; the more he could hold her the happier he was.

Sam and Jill lived this way for several months in the small travel trailer until they decided to approach Robin and again ask for help. "We want to buy a mobile home and need you to cosign for us," Sampson told his mother. They had been looking around and found a nice, three-bedroom, two-bath home that was offered at a great price. Since they promised that they could make the payments, Robin caved and agreed to cosign, but she would not allow them to set up the home on Jill's grandmother's property. Robin owned a five-acre mini-ranch with a nice home and barn that housed the boys' quarter horses. She had Sam fence off one acre and put in a septic tank and an electric pole. They ran pipes from a deep well that they could share as it was in the middle of both properties.

Jill and Sam's new home was delivered and set up within three weeks. Sam was very happy, but Jill did not have much to say. This time she did not get her way and obviously did not like it. But she seemed relieved to be out of the tiny travel trailer. Robin was able to finance most of the mobile home, septic tank, and the electric and gas hook-ups with a sizeable down payment through a highly penalized distribution from her 401k. Jill and Sam brought their clothes and personal items to their new home. Robin bought them a service for four set of dishes, four water glasses, some pots and pans, and silverware. She gave them some of her sheets, and they were ready to go. Life was getting better for everyone. Even Jill seemed more content. "Thank you for all of this," she said to Robin.

Sam brought Laurel to visit his mother several times a week and to get a quick power nap. She was so precious. She was completely bald and wore a stretchy bow around her perfectly shaped head. He always explained that Jill needed to clean or catch up with laundry and was busy. "Okay with me," Robin would say. "Tell her I said hello."

Life was status quo for a short time. Robin did not visit Jill, and Jill did not visit Robin until one Saturday afternoon, after Robin went on a baby shopping spree. She bought Laurel a swing, a bouncy walker, some size

3 to 6-months clothes, and a little pair of shoes. Robin
hoped that by now, Jill would be more receptive to her
as Laurel's grandmother. Jill let Robin into the house
when she saw the presents. Robin could not believe her
eyes as she walked from the entrance into the living
room. The place was a total mess. There was virtually
no place to sit as the chair and couch were full of
clothes, dirty and clean mixed together. Damp clothes
hung from the ceiling fan to dry. Laurel lay naked on
the bare floor, and the whole place smelled like wet
dog and urine. The TV was blaring a soap opera and
dirty dishes were piled in the sink. Mind you, Jill was
home all day every day as they only had one car, and
she did not work outside the home. Sam continued to
work two minimum-wage jobs just to make ends meet.
Robin asked for a diaper and put it and a new outfit
on the baby, gave her a kiss, and turned around and
walked out.

About three months later, Jill came over to Robin's
house hysterically crying. She was pregnant again. "I
can't handle this," she cried. "I don't think I can love
another baby. I hate my life, and I hate your son. This
is all your fault, you know. If you hadn't interfered in
our life, we would be far away from you!"

Later that night, Sam came over. With his head in
his hands, he said, "Mama, what am I to do? Jill is

so unhappy and blames me for everything." He cried. "She does not want this baby and is very depressed. I am afraid she will hurt herself, and I am afraid she will not take care of Laurel." Sampson decided that it was time to tell his mother the secrets that he had been holding in for so many years. He told her about the abuse that Jill had suffered at the hands of her father since she was eight years old and that when she tried to tell Lesa Mae, her mother either did not believe her or blamed her for leading Pete on.

Robin did not know what to tell her son. She decided to go to their house every day and try to help Jill cope with the pressures that she felt. Robin spent the next weekend cleaning their house, doing laundry, and changing the bedding in the crib and their bed. She helped Jill into the shower and helped her dress in clean shorts and a pretty shirt. After brushing her hair, Robin took Jill and Laurel outside for some sunshine and started supper. Robin called Jill's doctor, and the nurse said they would call in a mild antidepressant to the local pharmacy, and they wanted to see her the following week.

Between the daily help, the prescription, and Sam's undying love and support, Jill and Sampson survived the pregnancy and had another beautiful daughter. Mia McDaniel-Perez weighed seven pounds two ounces,

THE SYSTEM • 39

and was twenty inches long. She was perfect, totally bald like her sister, with a nice little round head and beautiful eyes. Another blessing from God. The one thing that Jill and Sam got right was having beautiful babies. Again, Jill chose not to nurse her daughter. Sam was good with this as it gave him quality time with his new baby at night and early in the morning, before he had to go to work.

Robin and Sam convinced Jill that she needed help to get over her depression and Jill agreed to see a Phycologist. The first visit was promising and, along with the antidepressant, seemed to lighten Jill's mood. The second visit did not go so well as the psychologist started delving into Jill's true feelings of love/hate for her father and her desire to have their special relationship back. She refused to go for a third visit. "He is a quack!" she said. "He thinks I still want to be special with daddy."

Jill, unable to cope with a fifteen-month-old who was walking and getting into everything, as well as a new infant called her mother for help. Jill's mother jumped at the chance to see her grandchildren and to get out of the house and away from her husband and other daughter. It was 4-H season again, and they were always in the barn working on the show steer or spending time together, planning their winning strategy. Lisa Mae was either oblivious to their special relationship or preferred to ignore it. One thing that Lisa Mae was really good at after running a large household and taking care of young siblings in her youth was organizing a house. She quickly got the recurring chaos organized, the children bathed and into clean clothes, and the laundry washed, folded, and put away in the proper places. The dishes were washed and the kitchen put back in order. Jill got to sleep in, and Sam was ecstatic! The mobile home had three bedrooms, so Jill's mother had her own room and shared a bathroom with Laurel. He went to work each morning knowing that his home and little girls were in good hands. Jill even admitted that she could indeed love another child. Was the Lord working in her life? When Jill and Sam needed a date night, Robin gave them enough money to go to a fast-food hamburger joint. Lisa Mae agreed to babysit and gave them money for a movie since she still worked at the store on Friday nights and Saturdays.

Then an unbelievable thing happened. Robin looked outside one Saturday morning, and standing in the yard, holding Laurel, was Jill's father. It seemed that Jill allowed him to come to see the children so that he would allow his wife to stay there longer. Jill, her father, sister, and brother were all in the yard, like one happy normal family. *Could this be really happening?* Robin wondered. *After so much time, so much drama, so much chaos? Were any of Jill's stories about the many years of abuse real, or was the whole thing the manipulative scam of a narcissistic, depressed, rebellious teenager?*

Sampson was working. Robin had to talk to him, so she called the grocery store first. Not there. She tried the hardware store, and he came to the phone. "What's wrong, Mama? Are my babies all right?"

"We need to talk, son, what time are you coming home?"

When Sam got home, he came right over to his mother's house, and Robin filled him in on the Stone family visit. He could not believe his ears. He immediately went to his trailer to confront Jill. Lisa Mae was in the kitchen with Jill when Sam came in. "How could you do this?" he yelled. "How could you let your child-molesting father in my house and let him hold my daughters?"

This was the third time that Lisa Mae had heard about the accusations made by Jill several years ago, but this time, someone else was making the accusations. She angrily told Jill she would not stay there another second. "You are a liar. You lied to me, and you lied to Sam. You have always been a hateful child, even after

everything we have given you!" Oddly enough, she did
not have a heart attack, despite her husband's warnings
many years before. The Stone family visit opened the
doors to reactions and emotions in everyone.

After Lisa Mae left her oldest daughter's home,
she started to think back over the past ten years. She
admitted to herself that she did not pay a lot of attention
to her daughters as they, especially Jill, were always
hanging out with Pete. Lisa Mae was not the least bit
interested in animals, especially steers. She thought
the whole 4-H thing was a waste of time and took so
much money away from the family's needs. Could it
be that Jill was telling the truth? Were the signs there,
and she just missed them. Or worse, had she chosen to
ignore the strange feelings she sometimes got in the pit
of her stomach. But Pete treated his girls so well. They
seemed so close; were they too close? Lisa Mae never
loved Pete. Actually, she never really even liked him.
He was her way out of the home she was raised in.
*Did he really molest Jill, and is he now hurting Kelly
in the same way?* she wondered. She needed a plan, a
plan to leave Pete and take Kelly and Pete Jr. with her.
Jill and her daughters had Sampson and a nice house.
She would be fine; she was a survivor. Lisa Mae would
escape, but she could not find a way to confront Pete.

Lisa Mae's plan was to get a full-time job and save

her paycheck to pay for her escape. She told Pete that she wanted to help with expenses. As the children were older and in school, she wasn't really needed during the day at home. Pete, seeing the advantages to this, agreed, and Lisa Mae started looking for another job. She quickly found a full-time position job at another convenience store that just opened right in town. The manager needed help and trained her to run the register, stock the shelves, and make a list of items that were getting low in quantity and needed to be reordered. She also made sandwiches to put into the cooler for the hungry lunch crowd who came in every day. Any leftover sandwiches were taken home at the end of the day and served for dinner, which saved money to put into the escape pot.

Because Lisa Mae did not have any real friends, she started visiting Jill again. She missed her grandbabies a lot, and this was her way of seeing them and perhaps getting a better idea of the truth. Jill, suffering from a new onset of depression, grew closer to her mother as she did not have any friends either, and she and Sam were either arguing or not talking since her father's visit.

Sam told Robin of Jill's continued depression. She did not want to get out of bed or off the couch, and she would not get dressed. After talking it over with Jill, Robin made another appointment with a female psychologist she knew from the hospital who did private consultations. Surprisingly, Jill agreed to see her. But after three sessions, she was done. The psychologist made Jill really angry by telling her that perhaps she was, "all about me," and that she needed to think about her children's needs. She prescribed another antidepressant and tried to schedule more visits, but Jill refused. "I don't need some shrink telling me what to do," she said. "I think I will do like my mother and find a job," she told Sam. "Then you could go to one job and keep the kids while I get out of this house." Sam was still very much in love with Jill and his precious daughters, so he agreed.

There was another opening at the store where Lisa Mae worked, and the manager agreed to hire Jill. She was a quick learner, and together they made an efficient team and could work alternating shifts if necessary. Sam was happy working one job and being with his daughters, and Pete was happy with his newfound freedom to do as he pleased. Robin was cautiously optimistic with growing hope that her prayers for harmony were being answered. "I trust you, Jesus, and thank you in advance for the work you are doing in our lives."

Joe Harvy was a deliveryman who brought supplies

to the store where Lisa Mae and Jill worked. He was forty-two years old with blond, wavy, thick hair and blue eyes. He was five feet eleven inches tall and had a basically trim build except for a little potbelly that hung over his belted uniform pants. His good looks and charismatic personality made him instantly attractive to both Lisa Mae and Jill. Joe wore a strange ankle bracelet that was black, two inches in diameter, and appeared to have a permanent locking mechanism. It hung low, past the cuff of his pants and above his shoes. Joe and Lisa Mae quickly formed a friendship. They drank coffee and ate a sandwich on her breaks. Their friendship turned into a more interesting relationship. But they could not officially date as she was still married, and he had to be in his apartment by dark every night.

After getting to know Joe better, Lisa Mae asked him about his unique ankle bracelet. He explained that he was on house arrest for some trouble he had gotten into a year ago. It seemed that he was "wrongly" accused of having an inappropriate encounter with his ten-year-old daughter, and his ex-wife pressed charges. Although a he said/she said unprovable charge, based on the accounts of his daughter, Joe was found guilty and placed on house arrest for five to eight years, depending on probation and the appeal system. Yes, another pervert who apparently liked tender-aged girls. He swore to Lisa Mae that he was totally innocent of these bogus charges, and that his rebellious daughter was acting out against him grounding her for talking back and saying bad words to her teacher. Because Lisa Mae spent several years dealing with the rebellious Jill, she could relate to his explanation. And besides, he was so attractive.

Lisa Mae had not noticed that Jill was also attracted to Joe. She flirted with him behind her mother's back and found reasons to stand close to him as he stocked his supplies or went to the back storeroom. Joe reminded Jill of a blond version of her father: same age, height, weight, little potbelly, wavy hair, and he possessed an air of confidence and swagger. Jill did not care about the house arrest and decided to take him up on his offer to move into his apartment. She moved out of her home with Sam that weekend. Sunday night she called Sam to tell him she wanted a divorce. They could share the girls as she wanted a divorce settlement where neither of them had to pay child support and had shared custody. She would keep them on Medicaid for their health care, and she would apply for Medicaid assistance also. She told Sam about Joe's house arrest but did not believe he was guilty of such charges. Jill was sure her mother would understand, and they both could keep their jobs. She had it all worked out. She would have her way!

Sampson was devastated. He knew that Jill was unhappy, still depressed, but they could work it out. They had been through so much through high school. Hadn't he done everything she asked? Now she was gone. "Please come back home. I can forgive you, and we can put our family back together. Just come home," Sam begged. Jill laughed to herself. Sam was so predictable and so idealistic. He would do exactly what she wanted.

What Jill did not consider in her plan was the bond between Sam, his children, and his mother. When Robin heard Jill had moved out of her home and her demands, she and Sam consulted a lawyer. "We have to get legal advice, Sam. We have to protect Laurel and Mia from both of these sick men and from their own mother," Robin said.

"You are right, Mama," Sam admitted. He also expressed how much he still cared for Jill and how much he really wanted to help her. But he loved his babies more and would give his very life for them. He told the lawyer, Ho Vu, about the charges against Jill's new manfriend, his ankle bracelet tracker, his curfew, and his house arrest. They discussed the suspicions against her father.

Mr. Vu was a third-generation Florida-born native. He was a small, well-built man of about fifty years old. He owned a small cattle ranch with Black Angus stock and two cow ponies just outside of Maverick. He was considered one of the "cowboys" throughout the tri-county area and was well respected and liked by the locals, law enforcement, and the judges who sat in the county courthouse. Mr. Vu was a married man with two small children. He exhibited a confident and pleasant way that gave Sam and Robin a good feeling.

Sam wanted protection for his daughters from these potential dangers. What were his rights? What were his children's rights? Mr. Vu told Sam and Robin about the Florida Department of Children and Families (DCF), who worked in partnership with local communities to promote strong families and to protect the vulnerable. Their goals were to provide services with integrity and accountability. Mr. Vu encouraged them to contact the DCF and explain their particular circumstances. DCF caseworkers usually represented mothers and looked into potential or actual danger from the father or male partner in the relationship, creating an atmosphere where children are vulnerable. Mr. Vu gave Sam the names of other agencies that provided protective services but told us these agencies were predominately reactive, not proactive. Mr. Vu further explained that until custody was assigned by the courts, both parents had equal rights to the children. He asked permission to start proceedings to assign temporary custody to Sampson with visitation rights for Jill. The system would not deny visitation by either parent and would not allow Sam to withhold visitation. But the courts would weigh the circumstances and could assign supervised visitation if deemed appropriate. He told us that the courts usually favored the mother in these situations. He agreed to represent Sam for a modest retainer, which he would hold in escrow until a court date was set.

Robin could see that Sam was overwhelmed by his circumstances. After praying with him to trust in Jesus, she decided to send him and his children on a brief vacation. Robin had a good friend who owned a cabin on a lake that she could rent for two or three weeks. She rented it for three weeks so that Sam could have the extra weekends to chill and regroup. Robin's friend did not charge them any rent as she was also a good Christian woman who could not tolerate any form of child abuse.

Sam did not tell Jill where they were going, which turned out to be a big mistake. One day while Robin was at work, Jill sneaked on to the property and went into their mobile home to look around. She found that most of Sam's, Laurel's, and Mia's clothes were gone. "What is this? Sam moved out of here and has taken my children with him?" She became infuriated. Losing control, Jill began to destroy the mobile home. She broke furniture, scratched the cupboards and countertops with a butcher knife, dented the stove and refrigerator, dumped ketchup and mustard on the kitchen floor, and broke all the glasses and dishes. When she found their wedding album, she took a butcher knife to the face of every picture of Sam, cutting his face to shreds. Before leaving, she wrote a note: "I will find you, and I am going to take you for everything you have!"

Jill looked around and decided she could not do anymore damage to the inside of the house. So she went to her truck and found a baseball bat. She proceeded to pound the outside of the mobile home with the bat, leaving over twenty dents in its exterior. Still not satisfied with her destruction, and still in an uncontrolled rage, she took an axe to the outside of the trailer and hacked multiple large holes in the siding. When her rage was finally satisfied and after apprising her work, she left. "That will teach you not to mess with me," she said aloud.

When Robin came home, she noticed that the gate was open and began to look around. When she found all the damage, she called the police. The police arrived and made a report, but unless she could prove Jill did the damage, she could not press charges against her. Jill had not signed the note, and the note on its own was not enough proof. And since the trailer were in both Sam's and Jill's names, she had the right to enter it. She did not, however, have the right to enter Robin's property. The police explained that to stop Jill from entering her property, Robin would have to catch her on the property, give her a verbal "no trespassing" warning, and then catch her a second time on the property, detain her, and call the police. But with this show of violence, there was zero chance that Robin would be able to follow those instructions. This was how the system worked.

Robin called Sam. "You need to come home. Jill is out of control, and we need to deal with this head-on." When Sam and the children came home, he was faced with this mess. Robin had taken pictures and documented the damage for future use. Sam took this information and copies of the pictures to Mr. Vu. He just filed them away and shook his head.

Sam and the girls stayed with Robin as they cleaned up and restored their home to a state of near normalcy. The counters had to be restored, and the siding had to be replaced. Thank God that Sam could do most of this work himself, with the help of some friends. Robin was still taking a class or two working toward her advanced nursing degree but decided to put her classes on hold and work as much overtime as she could to help with expenses and attorney's fees. Sam would stay home with his daughters and work only on the weekends that Robin was off. "I don't get this, Mama. How could Jill be so out of control?" Sam asked. Sam recognized Jill's and Joe's trucks driving by from time to time. But they did not try to contact him or visit the girls.

It did not take long to get a court date at the county courthouse. Jill was able to get a court-appointed public defender. Sam and Mr. Vu were to report to the courthouse at ten o'clock. Mr. Vu met Sam and Robin there at 9:30 and briefed Sam on what he needed to tell the judge. Mr. Vu and Jill's attorney had previously submitted their petitions to the clerk of court.

Robin was in the gallery to support Sam. Jill's father, mother, and Joe sat on the opposite side of the gallery. The judge told Jill and Sam that he had read the documents. He asked each of them if they had anything to add. Jill began to sob violently. Through her tears, she said, "I just want my babies back." The judge asked her where she and her children would live. She replied that they would live in the apartment she shared with her boyfriend. "They would be safe there with me, their mother."

It only took the judge a second to respond. Pounding his gavel, he ruled that both children would temporarily reside with their father in the mobile home in Maverick. He further ruled that Jill could have liberal and frequent visitation at the discretion of their father, and that Sam would be present at and supervise each visitation. The judge ruled that the DCF conduct an investigation and report their findings to him in one month.

The case decided, at least temporarily, everyone departed the courtroom and did not speak. Mr. Vu, Robin, and Sam met briefly at the lawyer's office to discuss the terms of the judge's ruling and to discuss Jill's first visit. The Stone family, including Joe, met at the local diner to discuss the judge's findings and their next move. "This is just not fair. That stupid judge doesn't know what he is talking about! These are my children, and I want them back," Jill exclaimed. Pete and Joe nodded in agreement. Lisa Mae just listened and did not say a word.

Jill called Sam that night to set up a visitation for the following Saturday morning. She told him that she agreed the girls would be better off with him for now, and she would like to visit with them outside the house and not on the porch. "Can we meet in the driveway?" she asked politely. He agreed to this arrangement and to put Zorro in his large pen outside.

Robin had a really bad feeling about this arrangement as her corner property was surrounded by dense woods with large oak and pine trees and many bushes. There was a dirt road on two sides of the property, just a few yards beyond the woods. "Sam, please don't trust this woman. She can be very manipulative and sneaky."

"Don't worry so much, Mama. Jill just wants to visit with Laurel and Mia. It will be fine." Robin notified the sheriff about the pending visitation and that the Stone family had a potential for violence, as noted by the previous destruction of Sam's home, though charges were not filed due to lack of evidence. The sheriff took note of the time and place and assured Robin that he would send a deputy to patrol the area on Saturday morning.

On Saturday, Sam pulled his pickup next to Robin's house at the near end of the driveway, filled a small cooler with ice and a few cold drinks, and prepared his mind for the visit. He was actually looking forward to reuniting his family and secretly hoped that when Jill saw how well the girls were doing and how happy

THE SYSTEM • 55

baby Mia was, she would stop this foolishness and come home.

Jill was right on time. She pulled up to the other end of the driveway on the lime rock road, got out of her car, and walked toward Sam, Laurel, and Mia. Jill was dressed in tight denim cutoffs and a low-fitting tank top; she had flip-flops on her feet. Her dark hair was newly cut in an attractive bob. "You look good," Sam said.

Jill smiled as that was the exact response she wanted from Sam. "Thanks," she replied. *You are so predictable.* she thought. *Daddy's plan is going to work perfectly, and I will get my children back.* After a brief conversation with Sam, Jill started chasing Laurel around the yard. Laurel loved the game and squealed with delight. They ended up close to the end of the driveway. Jill left the game and came back to Sam's truck to pick up Mia. As soon as she picked up the baby, she hollered, "Now!" Her father ran from the bushes, where he had been hiding, snatched Laurel and ran with her to a truck waiting for him on the side road. He and Laurel jumped in, and they sped away. He had a shotgun in one arm and Laurel in in the other. At the same time, Jill, with Mia in her arms, kicked off her flip-flops, cleared the side fence, and ran to a second waiting truck. "Drive!" she yelled at the man behind the wheel, and they sped off in the opposite direction from the first truck. A third man in a truck also sped off, spitting lime rock from his oversized tires as he left the scene.

Sam was in shock. All three drivers were male and wore matching baseball caps pulled low over their faces. This plan to kidnap the girls had been precisely planned and executed. Overwhelmed, Sam jumped in his pickup and sped out of the driveway. But he did not know which truck to follow. He panicked; he did not know what to do. In just a few split seconds his precious baby girls were gone.

Finally, he randomly picked one of the trucks and chased it through Maverick. When they came in front of the county courthouse, Sam saw an opportunity to force the driver off the road without wrecking the truck and possibly hurting his babies. The driver did exactly as he planned, and veered off into the courtyard. Sam jumped from the truck, snatched his shotgun from the gun rack, and ran to the other truck's window. Jill's father looked at him and smirked. "You chose wrong, boy!" Just before he left the road, he transferred Laurel to the third truck, where Lisa Mae was waiting in the passenger seat.

Pete laughed until he saw the shotgun. For a fleeting moment, Sam contemplated pulling the trigger on this man for everything he had done to the woman he loved, and now this! But his conscience and God's intervention spared Pete's life.

Jumping back into his truck, Sam raced through the town, continuing to search for his babies. Because he was driving so fast and had his shotgun in his gunrack, a patrolling deputy stopped him. It was the same deputy who promised to patrol Robin's house that morning but had not shown up. A second deputy pulled up, flanking Sam's truck. "Stop your car, roll down your window, and toss out the keys," the officer commanded. "Now put your hands on the steering wheel where I can see them," the second deputy yelled. They detained Sam but did not cuff him. Both deputies recognized Sam from the Maverick High School football games.

Sam was obviously very upset. "Please let me go," he begged. "They kidnapped my babies. They have guns and are very bad people. I have to find my babies and keep them safe." Sam told them about the danger that Laurel and Mia were in and how he was tricked by their mother and her perverted father and boyfriend. Sam told the deputies about the three trucks and about expecting them to patrol the area.

They detained him until he calmed down and then let him go. "Go directly back to your house, and we will be there shortly." When the sheriff's deputy got to the house, he took Sam's statement.

Robin was beside herself. For the first time in her life, she felt completely helpless. "Where were you this morning? You promised to be here and did not show up! This is all your fault," she screamed at the deputy. She was unable to talk, unable to cry, unable to think, unable to pray.

Sam was also unable to function. He blamed himself for being so stupid. This was all his fault, and he did not know how to fix it. The deputies left after taking statements, promising to keep an eye out for the children and the Stone family. But they did not have much hope that they would still be in or around Maverick.

Sunday went by without either Sam or Robin being able to eat or sleep. As soon as Mr. Vu came into the office on Monday morning, he found Robin and Sam waiting for him. After hearing their horrible rendition of the events of the visitation, he wrote a petition and called the clerk of the court to schedule an emergency hearing. The hearing was scheduled for one o'clock. According to Mr. Vu, Judge Johnson was a no-nonsense judge, who was also a family man with a grandson. The judge read the petition during lunch, and after asking Mr. Vu a few questions, he told the clerk to issue an immediate emergency protective custody order in the names of Sampson McDaniel-Perez and/or Robin McDaniel for the two minor children, Laurel and Mia McDaniel-Perez. He also told her to alert the DCF and sheriff's offices in the tri-county area to put out an Amber Alert for Laurel and Mia. Judge Johnson instructed Sam to call the sheriff if he located the children, and the sheriff and DCF would take them into protective custody. "Do you understand these instructions?" Judge Johnson asked.

"Yes, sir," Sampson replied.

"We understand and thank you, sir." Robin said.

After leaving the courthouse, Robin and Sam went home to gather two recent pictures of Laurel and Mia. Sam quickly designed a flyer that stated "Missing Children" and contained their contact information with instructions to contact the sheriffs' offices or DCF if the children were seen. He took the draft to a print shop and had hundreds of copies made. Sam went to every electric and telephone pole as well as every store and business in the tri-county area and posted the flyers.

The father of a good friend from Sam's football days owned a private detective business. Sam contacted Mr. Evens, explained the entire sordid story, including the danger the children were in, and asked him if he would help him find Laurel and Mia. Mr. Evens agreed. He started an intense investigation into the extended families and addresses of relatives of the Stones and the Harvys. "You are the best, Mr. Evens. I can't tell you how desperate my mom and I are."

Around this time, the first set of phone calls started. During the day, when Sampson was off shift, he would just get to sleep and the phone would ring. "How does it feel to not know where your children are?" Jill would ask mockingly when Sam answered the phone. Although Jill was in her element by taunting Sam, she had really not thought out this whole scenario. Now she was actually stuck with two children, no home, no clothes or diapers, no formula, and no real help. Yes, her relatives would hide them for a short time, but they could barely meet their own needs, let alone feed and clothe three more people. Because Jill spent most of her time in bed or in front of the TV after having Mia, she never bonded with her and did not know how to care for an infant. This was harder than she thought it would be. She decided that she needed to call Sam again and have a little fun.

"I will find my babies, and you, your father, and boyfriend will pay if they have been hurt," Sam shouted into the phone.

She hung up the phone laughing. But Sampson was

a smart and attentive young man. He noticed that every time she called, there was a strange noise on the phone line when he answered. The noise was similar to a poor connection or static where reception was limited. Since his father had worked in the telephone industry, Sam knew it had to be specific to a rural or forest area. He set out on a mission to discover where Jill was calling from in hopes of it leading him to rescuing his beautiful baby girls.

He began calling town by town, listening carefully when the other end of the line was answered. Finally, he called a small town about an hour away. When the store clerk picked up the phone, there it was! The static! Now he had a heading. It appeared that she was always calling from the town of Alto.

These calls were highly disturbing, but they provided hope that the girls were close. Although Jill's family was very cunning and inventive, Mr. Evens was very good at finding people. After Sam told him what he had discovered, within two weeks, Mr. Evens had the addresses of several relatives and friends who lived in Alto and were likely to hide Jill and the children. He was able to narrow the possible relative to one residence in Alto, and it was a matter of staking out the home to determine if Jill and the children were inside. Mr. Evens biggest concern was if Sam found them first that he would not be able to follow the judge's stern instructions, so he did not call Sam right away.

Then early on Saturday morning, Mr. Evens spotted Jill, Laurel, and Mia heading back to an aunt's trailer after taking a walk. Mr. Evens alerted the sheriff and called the DCF. He then called Sam and his son and told them to meet at the DCF office. "Where are they? I need to be there," Sam said.

"Just do what I tell you, Sam," Mr. Evens instructed. "We must let the local sheriff and DCF do their jobs." "We must follow the judge's instructions."

The DCF representative, sheriff, and Mr. Evens knocked on the door and yelled, "DCF!"

Jill, shocked, opened the door, and she and the girls were taken into custody. "You can't do this. These are my children. I have rights," she screamed. The group proceeded to the DCF office, where the emergency protective custody order was read to Jill, who was still in the deputy's car. The children were separated from their mother and put into car seats in the DCF van. Jill denied knowledge of the order and claimed that she had the right to see her daughters. "I have done nothing wrong," she said and began to sob.

Sam and Mr. Evens' son arrived at the DCF office just as his daughters were taken out of the van. He immediately ran to his daughters and held them close, giant tears in his eyes and prayers of thanksgiving on his lips. He hugged Mr. Evens so tightly that the breath was hugged out of him. "How can I ever thank you, sir," Sam asked with sincerity.

"Seeing these little ones safe is all the thanks I need. I wish you all the best, son, and will be saying prayers for you."

As soon as he was able to, Sam called Robin, who shed tears of relief. "Thank you, Jesus. You are so good. Please forgive me for not trusting you. I fall so short."

Robin knew that they could not bring the children back to her home, so she contacted her friend Ruby, who had allowed Sam and the babies to spend their brief vacation at her lake house. Robin explained what was going on and asked if they could live there until the case was settled because they were afraid for their safety. "Of course. You can stay there as long as it takes. Consider it your safe house, and take care of your family. Let me know if you need anything at all."

Jill was detained at the DCF office to fill out some papers and give her statement. She was not allowed to use the phone, so her father and boyfriend were unaware of what just went down. The sheriff and DCF were aware of the alleged kidnapping and did not want any further trouble from Jill's family. These several hours gave Sam and Robin a chance to gather clothes, toiletries, bedding, two playpens, and food to take to the cabin. They were escorted to their new safe house by Mr. Evens and a deputy. You would think that Mr. Evens and his son were family as they were so happy.

It did not take long for the family to settle in to their new, small but comfortable home and resume their rotation of caring for Laurel and Mia. Robin's younger son, the horses, and cat were picked up by Big Sam for the summer. Zorro went with his babies and really loved the lake. He would run to the end of the dock and jump into the cool water. Zorro was delighted when Sam or Robin joined him and swam out to a large floating dock. Life would be good for the summer. They said prayers of thanksgiving and praise every night, the girls kneeling close to the bed with their little hands folded and heads bowed. The family sang songs like "Jesus Loves Me, This I Know" and "This Little Light of Mine" as they held hands and danced to the music.

Robin and Sam could only imagine the fury of Jill and her family. All visitations were suspended until another custody hearing. Mr. Vu petitioned the courts for a psychological exam for Jill and to determine the house arrest status of Joe Harvy. Mr. Vu did not want him to have any contact with the children when visitation was reestablished with their mother. DCF physicians found the girls healthy and happy. They enjoyed the constant attention of and playtime with their father and grandmother at the lake. Thank God they would probably not remember any of this.

Life for the McDaniel-Perez family returned to a state of normalcy at the lake cabin. They found a great little family-orientated church, in which Robin sang in the choir, that accepted them with open arms. Only the pastor knew the reason for their stay at the lake, and he promised to keep their secret.

Robin felt a sense of hope for the upcoming battle that she could only imagine would soon be coming their way. The courts, DCF, and the Partnership for Strong Families were all involved usually found in favor of the mother, so their case had to be well documented and strong. Mr. Vu wanted court-ordered supervised visitation for Jill and the children, but he was not confident in the system based on past experiences.

In the meantime, Jill and her mother rented an apartment together so it would look like Joe Harvy was out of the picture. Lisa Mae had separated from Pete and was considering divorce. Kelly and Pete Jr. continued to live with their father and attend school.

For many weeks there was no contact or visitation

allowed with Jill, and the children were tucked away safe and sound. Despite many attempts to follow Robin or Sam home from the hospital, their location remained unknown to the Stone family. The deputy had schooled them in the art of detecting a tail and how to circle repeatedly to avoid being followed.

After sixty days of peace, the dreaded court date was set. Sampson was to appear at ten o'clock on Wednesday morning. He kissed his precious girls and left early to meet with Mr. Vu. Jill and her attorney were there. She looked very respectable, dressed in a nice skirt, modest blouse, and low pumps, and she carried a matching purse. After reviewing the case, the judge asked Jill about her relationship with Joe Harvy. She denied a continued relationship with him, stating that she lived with her mother and that they both held jobs in the same store on the outskirts of Maverick. "I don't see him or my father anymore," she lied. Mr. Vu presented his case based on Jill's past disregard for her children's safety and exposure to potentially dangerous and violent family members and friends. While Jill took out a tissue and wiped her teary eyes, her attorney stated that she regretted her past actions and begged the court to grant her visitation. "My mother can be there with me if the courts will agree. I miss my baby girls so much," she stated.

The judge, finding Jill sincere and with her mother agreeing to be present during visitations, granted her visitation every Saturday between 9 a.m. and 5 p.m. She could take the children shopping or to the playground. "You are not to have any contact with your father or ex-boyfriend when you have the children," the judge instructed. He also ordered that Sam was to take the children to the apartment, drop them off with Jill or Lisa Mae, and pick them up there.

As Jill was working full time at the store, the judge ordered her to start paying a modest amount of child support to assist with the care of her children, and she agreed. The judge ordered the payments to be sent to Sam on the first of every month via a personal check, cashier's check, or money order. Jill's and Sam's attorneys were to set up the contract, and payment would commence within two weeks. "Two hundred dollars a month is a lot of money. I don't make much at the store," Jill complained but was cautioned to be silent by her attorney.

Laurel was twenty months old and running around, getting into everything. Mia was starting to crawl, so they required a lot of close attention. Robin and Sam prayed for their safety every time that they were with their mother. Lisa Mae would be there to keep an eye on things.

This routine went on Saturday after Saturday with no apparent issues for about six weeks. Jill usually returned the girls dirty and hungry, sometimes with minor scrapes and bruises from playing in the playground but generally unharmed. Until about 3 p.m. one Saturday Sam got a call from the ER. One of Sam's coworkers worked an opposite shift from Sam in the same ER and recognized Laurel and Mia. Lisa Mae had noticed something wrong with Laurel after coming home from a shopping trip. The children had been bathed and were already in the apartment. Laurel was pouting and moving awkwardly, unusual for her. So under the pretense of wanting to take them for ice cream, she decided to have Laurel checked out in the ER. She had suspicions that Jill had been secretly seeing Joe and that he was joining her in the playground when she had the girls. She also suspected that Joe had been in the apartment during this visitation. He was still under house arrest and was wearing his ankle bracelet, but he was allowed to be out when driving to and from work and while at work.

When Lisa Mae arrived at the ER, she explained that she was the grandmother, and the children were under the protection of DCF. The ER staff could not examine Laurel or Mia without a DCF representative there and without the custodial parent giving permission.

After getting the call from his friend at the ER, Sam was extremely upset and called Robin. "Mama, please drop everything and come with me. I think there may be a problem with Laurel. She is at the ER with Lisa Mae." Robin and Sam made it to the ER in record time, just before the DCF representative. When all parties were present, the girls were taken to a room, and Laurel was questioned about who was there when she visited her mother. Laurel, being so young, said that there was a man there, but she was an unreliable witness. She did not know his name and tired quickly of the question-and-answer game. She was given a brief exam, during which some old bruises on her knee were found and some redness in other areas. As she was freshly bathed, and smelled like lotion, the redness could have been a skin reaction to it.

The DCF representative recommended a full examination and physical to be conducted at a future date by a nurse specialist hired by the agency. Sam would be notified when the appointment was set. He was told to take the girls home and that they would call him regarding next week's visitation. "Thank you for looking after the girls," Sam said to Lisa Mae. She nodded and smiled.

Sam and Robin learned that DCF representatives are very special people who are invested in providing care to families with the goal of family reunification when possible. Sam and the girls were also involved with the Department of Children's Protection (DCP), which is responsible for many other services that involve families and children. Thus, its focus may be divided into multiple areas. Children, like Laurel and Mia, assigned to DCP are given case numbers and assigned caseworkers. When Sam asked why his girls had several caseworkers, the current one explained to him that each assigned caseworker has a specialty area, so when a child's needs change, the caseworker also changes. Laurel and Mia had already had three caseworkers, who had only the written records to pull information from. Verbal communication seemed to be a challenge, and priority was given to the children who were in immediate danger or were being blatantly abused. She explained, "Your children are in a safe, comfortable home where they have plenty of food, clean clothes, and your love and attention. They are smart, cheerful children who are developmentally and socially exactly where they need to be." "This is how the system works."

The physical assessment appointment was set up for two weeks from Monday at the large university teaching hospital where the team from the DCP worked. All visitations with Jill were cancelled pending the results of the assessment by the nurse specialist. She was a very professional but gentle woman of about fifty years of age. She had a soft soothing voice that the girls responded to easily. Robin drove the girls to the hospital, and Sam followed in his car. Though Jill was prohibited from being at the hospital, Sam was afraid that she or her family might try to interfere. This precaution turned out to be unnecessary because they were either not there or hiding in the parking garage. Either way, Robin got the children safely into the hospital lobby area, where she was met by the DCF social worker. They waited for Sam to arrive and then headed to the examination area, where each child was examined thoroughly. After two weeks at home, good care, and gentle bathing, there were no signs of redness or bruising on either Laurel or Mia. The nurse specialist determined that the exam was normal and negative for any issues. The social worker had no option but to reinstate Saturday visitations with Jill.

"Divorced. I am now divorced. Mama, in less than three years, I graduated from high school, got married, had two beautiful daughters, bought a nice home, and now I am divorced. I have been such a fool! Now I have two precious children to take care of and to try to keep safe, and my back is up against a wall. I don't know how to do this. We keep praying for strength, wisdom, and guidance, but this ordeal seems to be endless. I feel like I take one step forward and two steps back," Sam complained to his mom.

"I know, honey. We need to have a plan to get you out of this vicious circle. God has had our backs so far, and your children have been kept from being harmed. We just have to trust him. You said you regret not going to college. What do you think about taking some night classes? You have mentioned several times that you would really like to become a paramedic. With some of your dual-enrolled classes from high school, you already have your associate of science degree, and with your ER experience, I think you could get right into the program. We can juggle the children, and you should be able to still work part time." Within a few weeks, Sampson was accepted into the paramedic program and seeing a light at the end of his tunnel.

Jill's attorney and Mr. Vu worked out the divorce paperwork. All previous rulings of the court were honored. Primary residence and custody remained with Sam. Saturday visitation remained in force but with the provision that Saturday visitation could be waived if either party wanted a break. The waived visit required a two-week notice from either party. The child support payment remained the same, $200 per month. The judge did not seem to notice that Jill had never made a payment as previously ordered.

Sam was not the only one who had gotten a divorce. Lisa Mae was in the middle of divorcing Pete. She left the apartment and moved with Pete Jr. back to the house where she was raised. Her parents were both dead, and the farm was overgrown and unworked. But the house was in good shape. Pete Jr. enrolled in a different school, where he was immediately accepted on the track and cross-country teams. He was very was happy to be the center of his mother's attention again. Pete was to pay Lisa Mae alimony and child support, and she soon found a job at a local store. Life was good for Lisa Mae and Pete Jr. Soon after Lisa Mae moved back home, she started seeing her second cousin. They had remained friends throughout her marriage to Pete. They got along so well as children, and their friendship grew stronger now. After about a year, they decided to get married. Lisa Mae's new husband was a Church of Christ pastor, and both Lisa Mae and Pete Jr. became born-again Christians. They never returned to Maverick.

After Sam and Jill's divorce was final, she moved back in with Joe Harvy. He was still on house arrest and would be for another six years. But Jill did not care. She had him leave their apartment when she got Laurel and Mia on Saturdays. Or so she said. She knew that no one would check; DCF was too busy with real cases. Knowing that Sam was going back to school and would soon have a great job as a paramedic prompted Jill to start taking a class at the community college. She would apply to the police academy and become a cop! *I will make their lives miserable.* Jill did not make it into the police academy, but she took enough classes to qualify as a correctional officer. She got a job as a guard in the women's prison in a larger town near Maverick. Evidently vetting for a job as a correctional officer or prison guard was not as strict as for a cop. Sam and Robin could not understand how a woman, now married to a convicted felon still on house arrest, could be allowed to carry a gun and nightstick, and get a job in a nearby prison. *What kind of a legal system would even consider such a thing?* they wondered. Jill could be seen all around the town of Maverick in full uniform, weapons on her hip, even when she was not on duty. "Well, maybe now she will pay you some child support," Robin told Sam.

As a paramedic serving the tri-county area, Sam soon became very popular with the sheriff's department and the voluntary fire department. He and Robin were basic life support (BLS) instructors, and they gave free classes to the deputies and volunteer firefighters.

Every two years, the BLS certification by the American Heart Association (AHA) had to be renewed. Sam would borrow the adult, child, and infant mannequins from the AHA office, and he and Robin provided these woman and men their required recertification classes. As each instructor could officially only train six students at a time, Sam often got other BLS instructors to help with these classes. Their students were such fun that there was no problem getting his peers to help. The students brought in big sandwiches, chips, and cold drinks for a break during the classes, an added bonus.

One evening Sam came home from a twenty-four-hour shift and brought Laurel and Mia over to Robin's house. "Can you feed the girls, Mama? I am not feeling too well."

Sam seldom got sick. Robin couldn't even remember the last time he had a common cold. "What seems to be wrong?" Robin asked.

"Mama, I have a sharp pain in my right side, and I think I have a fever. It hurts really bad, and I threw up my lunch." Robin had him lie on the couch. When she pushed on his lower abdomen, he yelled out in pain. Robin diagnosed an acute appendix flare-up. Robin said she would feed the girls, but he needed to go to the ER. After a mild protest and another episode of pain and nausea, Sam was ready to go. They all piled into Robin's car and headed out.

When they got to the ER, where Sam still worked part time, the nurses took him right in. The ER doctor examined him and agreed that he had an acute abdomen. The general surgeon on call came in, and Sam was scheduled for emergency surgery that night. The OR on-call team and on-call anesthesiologist came in, and early the next morning, he was in surgery. Sam's appendix was in bad shape but removed without incident. He was taken to the recovery room and admitted for twenty-three-hour observation. Robin took the sleeping girls home and took the rest of the day off. "Daddy will be okay, but he has to stay in the hospital for a few days. Let's go get some lunch and ice cream," she suggested to the girls.

By coincidence, or God's intervention would have it, Big Sam and Salvage Sal were also in the same hospital. Salvage Sal had some chest pain and called his friend, Big Sam. Big Sam drove him to the hospital on doctor's orders. Salvage Sal had been diagnosed with a cancer a year before. It started in his lungs and spread to other parts of his body. He was a long-term smoker and been known to chew tobacco and partake in a drink or two on a daily basis. He refused to give up these bad habits even though the smoking made him cough violently, and the alcohol was contraindicated with the chemotherapy he was getting every three days. Sal was in a private room on the fifth floor, the same floor that Sam was on.

When Robin came to visit the next morning, Big Sam recognized Laurel and Mia and came into Sam's room to investigate. He told Sam about Sal and took him into Sal's room. "What in the world are you doing here, Uncle Sal? I didn't even know you were sick," Sam asked.

After a big hug, and avoiding Sam's question, Sal told Sam about his gorgeous nurse. He immediately pushed his call bell to summon her. "Her name is Angel, and she is the prettiest and kindest nurse in the whole hospital," Sal said.

Salvage Sal was not exaggerating. Angel was a tall, curvy blonde with soft, dark-brown eyes and the most wonderful face in all heaven and earth. She moved with purposeful grace that was both efficient and professional but highly feminine. Sam was instantly in love. Angel was indeed the woman of his dreams. "Don't mess this up, boy," Sal said after he asked for a pain pill.

Sam needed a plan. He had never had a problem getting to know women before as they were attracted to his extremely good looks and sincerely charming ways. He was the ultimate gentleman and knew how to treat women. But he was out of practice with the past three years of stress and challenges. "Hi, my name is Sam, and I am in room 523, at the end of the hall. I had my appendix out early this morning and will be here for at least twenty-three hours. Uncle Sal is my close childhood friend. And Big Sam, his friend, is my father. They are very special to me," Sampson explained.

Angel smiled at him sweetly and told him that she had several very sick patients she had to attend to. "I will try to stop by later and look in on you, but if you need anything, just press your call bell."

When Angel came back on her rounds, Sam made his most convincing move. "I would like to meet you during a break for a cup of good coffee in the coffee shop. My treat." He gave her his best smile.

There was a definite attraction between them, so Angel agreed to come for him later that morning, when she took her break. After all, he needed to walk, and a cup of good coffee with a handsome man might be fun. Angel had married a man several years before at the request of her father. She did not love him, but as an obedient daughter, she married him. He knew that Angel was in nursing school and seemed to be threatened by her quest for higher education, so he tried to discourage this career path. Angel loved nursing and working with patients whom she could help during their healing processes or with their pain and discomfort, so she was determined to complete her education and pass her state licensing boards. She not only completed her classes but graduated at the top of her class. Angel aced her boards and was immediately hired by an elite private hospital.

The marriage did not work, and they were divorced a few months after her success at becoming an RN. The divorce was simple and equitable as there were no children and no property to settle. Angel was not interested in dating. She poured her time and energy into taking care of her patients, taking specialty classes at the hospital, and providing in-service programs to her peers. She spent her free time creating and making crafts, usually with her mother, and she donated them to her local church bazaars or gave them as birthday or Christmas presents to family and friends. But there was something about this man that she was very attracted to. *After all, it is only a cup of coffee,* she thought.

They walked down to the coffee shop and had a specialty brew, a latte with frothy whipped cream on the top. They shared a pastry that was warmed with melted butter. The coffee, pastry, and company were outstanding, and neither one wanted the break to end.

Sam was released later that day as his doctor was happy with his progress. Sam called his mom, who packed up the girls and drove in to pick him up. Angel's shift was over, and she stopped by to wish him a speedy recovery. As he waited for his mom, Angel pulled up a chair and chatted with him for a while. When she left, Sam walked to his uncle's room, said goodbye to Sal "You were right as usual, Uncle Sal, Angel is so great, and I am in love! He winked at Sal on his way out the door and home with Robin and his daughters.

Sam could not get Angel off his mind. He told his mom about Angel and asked her to order a single yellow rose to be sent to Angel at the hospital. The card said, "Thank you for having coffee with me. I would like to see you again. Please call." He included his phone number and signed it, "Hugs, Sampson McDaniel-Perez."

Angel received her flower surrounded by baby's breath and a pretty yellow ribbon. When she read the card, her heart fluttered a little. "I am acting just like a schoolgirl," she said to herself. She did not call until the weekend but finally gave in. "I would like to see you again. You seem like a really nice man. I will meet you for dinner, but I think we should go dutch." Sam agreed to a dinner date at a local mom-and-pop restaurant in Maverick as he was still had restrictions to his driving. They had a wonderful dinner of southern fried chicken with all the fixings. The dinner, location, and conversation were perfect.

Sam, deciding to test the waters, told Angel that he had primary custody of his two daughters and that they lived in a mobile home next door to his mom, who helped him with their care. He told her that they were two and three years old, and they were the lights of his life. Not wanting to scare her off, Sam did not tell Angel the circumstances of his having custody and primary residence. "Would you like to meet them someday? They are really great kids."

Angel, being directly from heaven, was excited to meet Laurel and Mia. "Let's take them on a picnic at a park in a couple of weeks, when you can drive. Maybe on a Sunday after church. I will pack a lunch, and you can bring the cold drinks," Angel replied.

Sam was so pleased that he sang all the way home, though he could not carry a tune. But he sang anyway. He was still singing when he told Robin about his date, their picnic plans, and how much he really liked Angel. Sam then called Uncle Sal and told him, "I haven't messed this up yet, Uncle Sal. You were right. Angel is truly a gift from God and came directly from heaven!"

Sam did not realize that his beloved Sal sounded weak and tired.

Sam healed rapidly and talked to Angel on the phone almost every evening since he was still off work for another week or more, depending on his post-op exam. The picnic was scheduled for two weeks from Sunday, and everyone was looking forward to it. Sam picked up Angel at twelve thirty and introduced her to Laurel and Mia. At three years old, Laurel was a beautiful, intelligent, and talkative little girl who definitely possessed her father's charm. She had long, straight, auburn hair that was pulled into a ponytail and tied with a pretty blue bow. Her eyes were a brilliant amber color, and her smooth skin was tan from playing out in the sun. Mia was also a beautiful little girl and a typical two-year-old. She was independent and did not want any help with her hair or her clothes. She pouted at the outfit that her dad picked out for her, and he finally relented. Mia was dressed in her favorite red shorts and purple T-shirt. Sampson did manage to braid her long blonde hair and tied a purple and red ribbon in it. How long that would last was an ongoing question. But for now, Mia was sure that she looked marvelous.

It was love at first sight when Angel met the girls. They helped her lay out the picnic blanket and peeked into the pretty basket to see what was inside. Angel had an assortment of sandwiches cut into triangles. She cut off the yucky crusts of the peanut butter and jelly, and had chicken salad on rye for her and Sam. Also in the basket were assorted healthy and unhealthy snacks, like potato chips and homemade French onion dip. There were apples and caramel dip and chocolate chip cookies. Sam brought juice, assorted soft drinks, and bottled water in a cooler filled with ice. He also brought paper plates, cups with spill-proof lids, and napkins. "This is the best picnic ever," exclaimed Laurel as Mia stuffed her little mouth with peanut butter and jelly triangles and nodded in agreement.

The four of them ate their lunch with the promise of cookies after they played on the slides, swings, monkey bars, and merry-go-round. Everyone was happy and tired at the end of the afternoon. "Mia and Laurel are great kids. No wonder they are the loves of your life," Angel said. "Where is their mother?"

Eventually, over the next several months, Sam told Angel about the bizarre circumstances that led to his custody of Laurel and Mia. He explained the issues he had with the system's inability to proactively protect his children from what they called "potential dangers." Sam further explained the DCF social workers highly favored the biological mother's rights to her children.

His ongoing battle had already lasted over three years with no resolution in site. Sam's greatest fear was based on his suspicions that Jill was ignoring the court orders and exposing their children to her husband and father. Sampson knew that he came with some pretty heavy baggage, but he was falling in love with Angel. And because he thought her feelings were the same, he knew he owed her knowledge of what she assuredly faced if they had a future together.

He was right. Angel also knew that she was falling in love with Sam, Laurel, and Mia. She and Robin got along great, and she was more than willing to back up this united team in every way that she could. Uncle Sal was right once again. Angel was sent from heaven.

Sampson proposed to Angel after they had been dating for about a year. They had a spectacular fairy-tale wedding at a popular garden in the area. The bride arrived in a horse-drawn coach. The draft horses were pure white and driven by a coachman dressed in a traditional topcoat with tails and a black top hat. Angel was accompanied by her father and her soon-to-be daughters. Sam waited with his best man and the minister under a canopy adorned with beautiful flowers When the coach came to a stop, Laurel and Mia got out with the help of the coachman and started down the aisle, the girls spreading rose petals and

THE SYSTEM • 85

looking absolutely precious in their flower girl dresses and a ring of flowers around their heads. First Angel's maid of honor came down the aisle, and the guests were asked to stand. Angel and her dad proceeded down the aisle to the traditional wedding song. Robin had tears in her eyes, but this time they were tears of hope and happiness. The ceremony was beautiful, and as vows were spoken and rings exchanged, a new future and a new family was started. "You have made me the happiest man alive, and I love you with all my heart," Sam whispered to Angel.

After a short honeymoon at the beach, life returned to normalcy. Jill continued to get the girls on Saturdays, until Laurel reported that her stepfather took them to lunch at the local hamburger place. "He is really funny, Daddy. And he likes to tickle us and make us laugh."

This news sent Sam into orbit. He had long suspected that Jill was not following the rules, and he called the DCF social worker in charge. She told Sam that they would not take the word of a young child and could not act without proof. "What proof?" Sampson yelled into the phone.

"You would have to have an eyewitness or pictures taken with a camera that shows dates of Joe Harvy with the children," the social worker explained. Again,

Sam called on the private investigator, Mr. Evans, for help. He agreed to follow Jill and the girls the next Saturday, but Joe did not show up. So much for normalcy!

To say that the Lord works in mysterious ways is an understatement. Jill called Sam to ask for the next two Saturdays off. "Daddy is in the hospital and is in really bad shape," she said. When Sampson asked what happened, Jill told him that Pete had been out running fence, and when he got to one of the gates, a storm suddenly came up. "He just had a few more yards to check when a lightning bolt struck the gate, went through his hand and arm, and grounded through his feet. Then a second bolt struck him while he was on the ground and blew out his spinal cord. Evidently one of his neighbors found him still lying on the ground several hours later and called 911. He is still alive, but the doctors said he will never walk again. They want to operate to stabilize his back so that he will be able to sit up. I guess I will have to help him after surgery."

To be completely honest, Sam and Angel did not cry about this news. They granted Jill's request to keep the girls home until further notice and immediately called Robin with the news. "Wow, that is some news. I am glad I tried to resist the tendency to be judge and jury in his case as I certainly don't want to be judged for my thoughts. But I can't honestly say I feel sorry for him," Robin admitted.

Pete had his surgery and was able to sit up in a chair several days post-op. He was in a lot of pain as he had steel plates, rods, and screws in his back. He was paralyzed from the waist down and had to have a catheter to drain his bladder. According to Jill, Daddy would have to spend several months in rehab, so she would have to look after all the farm animals and the dogs. Kelly would go to live with her mother and brother for quite a while because Jill refused to move her pretty younger sister into her apartment with Joe. Visitations were suspended for over a month, and Sam did not complain a bit. "Is it a sin to feel happy about this, Mama?" Sampson asked at a Sunday dinner. Robin could not answer, and he fully understood her non-answer.

Jill's visitations slowed down to two Saturdays a month. She spent more and more time with her husband as his house arrest restrictions were reduced to weekdays, and he could go up to fifty miles on weekends. They spent many weekends camping, going fishing, or going to cookouts at a friend's home. Two children would really put a cramp in their fun time.

This was great with Robin because she was able to give Sam and Angel a break. Robin had a timeshare at the beach, so she happily took Laurel and Mia there on many weekends. Both girls had swimming lessons last year at the YMCA, and after a few minutes at the shallow end of the pool, they were playing and having a ball. Despite living on a mini ranch and away from water, the girls were both highly athletic for their ages and confident in their abilities to swim. They all loved the beach and spent many hours making castles, being buried in the sand, and playing in the clear blue water. Robin took them waist high into the water so that they could jump high when the waves came in. Early in the morning and in the evenings, when it was cool, Robin walked the beach while the girls ran ahead. They thought it was really funny when they ran circles around their grandmother and left her in their dust.

Robin often sneaked out very early, while the girls were still asleep, and plant purchased shells along the beach in front of the resort so that the girls could find them and take their treasures home. "Look, Mom, we found thousands of pretty shells," they would exclaim to Angel.

One of Angel's talents was her ability to make seashell crafts. She and her mom made all kinds of innovative projects to keep Laurel and Mia entertained for hours after their trips to the beach. Sam painted a craft shelf for them to display their projects. Laurel's was her favorite color, blue, and Mia's was purple. The children were never aware that their family life was different. Because of Sam, Angel, and Robin, they felt loved, secure, and safe.

It was almost Mia's fourth birthday. She was growing up way too fast. This year she was going to have a big birthday party. Earlier that year, Sam and Angel purchased a nice home on the outskirts of Maverick. It was a three-bedroom, two-bath house with a nice closed-in back porch and a fenced-in yard. They had a gentle dog, Bubba, who was a yellow Lab mix, and a very vocal tabby cat, Kitty. It was the perfect place to have a birthday party. Sam, always going the extra mile, rented a bouncy house for Mia's friends to play in. Angel ordered her a special cake filled with colorful frosting balloons and lots of creamy icing. It was going to be such fun. They invited all the kids from Mia's Sunday school class.

Well, the best-laid plans sometimes don't work out too well. Laurel and Mia got up early, before their parents, and spotted the cake. They proceeded to wiggle it down off the counter and onto the floor with a splat. When Angel and Sam got up, they found both girls eating cake from the floor and covered with colorful frosting. They didn't know if they should laugh or get angry at the mess. The whole scene was so funny, as well as so tragic, that they ended up laughing after scolding the girls and putting them into the bath. What to do for a birthday cake was the next question. Angel called her mom, who she saved the day by whipping up a cake and decorating it with sprinkles and gumdrops. It was splendid, and the guests never knew the difference—until Sam spilled the beans to some of the parents.

Mia, having eaten a burger, chips, cake, and ice cream, announced that she was going to the bathroom. After she finished, she flushed the toilet and watched her donation swirl around and go down the small hole at the bottom. She then spied her toothbrush in the holder by the sink. The temptation was just too great as she wondered if it could swim. She tossed it into the toilet and flushed. The toothbrush did indeed swim, swirled around the bowl, and disappeared down the small hole at the bottom. It was gone! The next person to use the toilet had a big surprise as the toilet backed up, and water ran through the bathroom and out into the hall. The guest yelled for help, and Sam and Angel came running to see what the problem was. When Sam saw the flood, he immediately turned off the water at the valve behind the toilet. After trying to clear the obstruction with a plunger, he ended up having to take the whole toilet off. When he reached down the pipe, guess what he found. Yep, a small purple toothbrush. Angel and Sam had many adventures with their energetic daughters.

"I am the victim here," Jill exclaimed to the judge during another court appearance. Jill wanted unsupervised visitation for Joe Harvy when she had her visitation with Laurel and Mia. "We are a family, and he should be able to see and play with my children." Joe was over halfway through his house arrest and continued to wear his ankle-tracking devise. "He is a good man, Judge, and is innocent of the bogus charges from his daughter and ex-wife."

Mr. Vu was in the courtroom with Sam and confident that the judge would not allow this request. The judge would surely see that allowing direct contact with a man who was found guilty, wore a tracking device, and had several more years of confinement should not be a part of Laurel's and Mia's lives at this time. When he was proven right and the request denied, Jill left the courtroom in tears. "I am the victim, not you," she screamed at Sam on the courtroom steps.

Many years before, when Robin made the appointments for Jill to see two different psychologists, she was diagnosed as a dependent personality type with severe narcissistic tendencies. The phycologists both knew about Jill's long-time abuse as a child that lasted well into her late teens. One psychologist explained to Robin and Sam that Jill fit both diagnoses because she would not listen to anyone who did not see things her way. He further explained that "She has an excessive interest in only herself, her needs, and desires. This makes it almost impossible for her to acknowledge or pay attention to the needs of others. She sees the role of others as to provide her with praise, support, encouragement, and adoration. Jill's syndrome can, and probably will get worse if left untreated. And as time goes by, it could lead to an even more severe narcissistic personality disorder, where Jill will be driven by her needs and not understand or care about the feelings of others. She could be the terminal everlasting victim." This information could be given to Sam and Robin because Jill had signed a waiver when she started treatment. She had truly thought he would diagnose her as a victim and take her side.

A few months later, after the last unsuccessful court date, Jill announced that she and Joe were going to have a baby. They could barely pay their bills as Joe was behind in his child support, and Jill was helping him catch up. Jill had still not paid a cent of her assigned child support to Sam. She was going to have another girl. Laurel and Mia would have a new baby sister to play with when they came for visitation.

And when Joe was taken off house arrest, they could all play together. *This will be so great,* Jill thought. *And Sam and that interfering Robin cannot stop it.* She hated Robin so much. *She never did like me and did not want me to marry her precious son. I sure showed her!* Jill would have a baby who would love her and who she could love forever.

Joe was not pleased about another potential mouth to feed, but he did not say anything. After all, he got exactly what he wanted from Jill; she would do anything he said, and she was helping him with his delinquent child support so that he could hide some of his income for himself. With her help, he was able to leave the house on weekends. Life was good for Joe.

After Jill had her new baby, Laurel and Mia had a scheduled Saturday visitation. Their new sister was suffering with colic and cried all the time. The girls told their dad that they had to stay in the house with the crying baby and watch cartoons on TV. They soon got tired of this and asked to go home after a lunch of SpaghettiOs. Jill was happy to see them go, and Sam was glad to pick them up early. She was so tired; this was not what she imagined having another baby would be like. And Joe was no help at all. He would not hold the baby, and he did not want anything to do with Jill. "All she does is cry and eat, and you look

94 • KATHARYN DUNN

terrible," he told her. "How did I ever get myself into this?"

Joe had never been a one-woman man, and since Jill was getting older, he started looking around for a younger "friend" to hang with. He was still ruggedly handsome and could really turn on the charm, especially for young women who were just starting to look for a serious relationship. He had his freedom on the weekends, so he had time to shop around. He told Jill he was going to put in some overtime to help out. So, when Joe found a friend or two to spend some quality time with, Jill never suspected a thing.

When the new baby was about eight months old, Jill and Joe asked Pete, still in the nursing home, if they could move into his house on the farm. Jill was still taking care of the animals and had to go there every day. It was just too hard. Pete was soon to be moved to an extended-care facility and might never be able to take care of himself, let alone run a farm and care for animals, so he agreed. One or two at a time, Jill sold off the cow ponies and livestock. She used that money to pay the electric bills and buy food and clothes for herself, Joe, and the baby. Jill had quit her job just before the baby was born, but she needed to go back, so she could pay bills and support her new family while helping Joe with his child support and new truck payments. Her old Chevy was a bit tattered, but it was paid off, and Joe managed to keep it running. What Jill did not consider was the mortgage that Pete still owed on the farm, the homeowner's insurance, and the land taxes. After years of trying to contact Pete, the bank repossessed the land, and the government fought for its share of the back taxes. Jill, Joe, and their little girl were forced to move out. Once again Jill was a victim. "How could Daddy forget that he still owed money on the farm? It was all his fault!"

Pete was now on Medicaid and not doing well in the nursing home. He had developed complications due to his paraplegia that required several more operations. The fact that he could not feel much in his lower body was his only saving grace. Pete was a lonesome, bitter invalid who was paying the price for his transgressions. He had lost everything and destroyed many lives. Pete had no visitors in the nursing home. Jill, Joe, and the little girl found a trailer to rent in Maverick, took the dogs and a cat, and relocated.

That same year, Laurel started kindergarten. She was five years old and so very smart. This was one of the hardest things that Sam had to do for a long time. Taking his little girl to school and leaving her in the care of a stranger was very traumatic for him. Yes, he did go to parent-teacher meeting day and saw her classroom in the Maverick elementary school. The teacher had decorated the room with a jungle scene of trees, smiling lions, elephants, and friendly-looking natives who had brightly colored balloons with each child's name on them. Twelve children were scheduled to start kindergarten that momentous Monday, most accompanied by moms who, like Sam, had tears in their eyes. The teacher smiled knowingly and showed each new student to his or her assigned seats at one of the four round tables throughout the room. Laurel sat down and immediately picked up a crayon and started to color in the new coloring book with her name printed on the front. She did not even notice when her dad left the room. Sam blew his nose and wiped his eyes three times on the ride home.

Laurel excelled in her first year in school. She already knew her basic colors, could count to twenty-five without using her fingers, and could sing her ABCs. "Listen to my new song, Daddy. I can dance to it too," she exclaimed with proud delight.

Kindergarten seemed to fly by for Sam. His little girls were growing up too fast, and he wasn't sure he liked it. After summer vacation, Laurel would start first grade, and Sam would have to suffer through taking Mia to her kindergarten class. Sam had to meet with the school principal before leaving his daughters at school. They were still in his protective custody, and there were strict restrictions against their biological mother visiting or picking them up for any reason. He supplied the school with a release and pictures of Robin and Angel so that either of them could pick up the children. In addition, pictures of Jill and Joe were given to the principal and both teachers with strict warnings attached. Sam would have to continue this routine for the next few years as Jill was still getting Saturday visitations, and Joe was still on house arrest. Jill's visits were actually requested an average of two times per month; her time and attention were focused on her new daughter. After each visitation, Laurel and Mia were questioned at length about where they went and if Joe was with them. Sam continued to ask Mr. Evens to periodically keep an eye on the visitations. It appeared that Jill was keeping Joe away from all three girls. Did she know the truth about Joe? Was she afraid?

The same year that Laurel started kindergarten, Robin met the love of her life. She had gone on an annual vacation to the mountains with several of her nursing friends. They rented a large, five-bedroom, rustic cabin on the top of a mountain in Georgia. The log cabin had a large porch that overlooked a forest that was full of large oaks and colorful flowering bushes. The birds were a noisy attraction as they called to each other or sang their songs. The monarchs were everywhere, and although the women did not see them, they were sure there were deer and probably bears roaming around the forest. The owner of the cabin had garbage cans that were "bear-safe". On top of the mountain and in the cabin there was no cell phone reception, no landline phone, and no TV. The women did bring a boombox and music for sing-alongs and dancing. It was paradise. Robin and three of her friends were the more adventurous of the group and scheduled three whitewater rafting excursions in Georgia and the Carolinas. On the second rafting trip, they had a hunk of a guide, and Robin instantly fell in love with him. His name was Will, and the attraction was mutual. Will was an ex-marine who maintained his muscles and flexibility by working as a rafting guide and regular trips to the gym. After the rafting trip, Will and Robin agreed to meet at one of the dance clubs in a small town at the bottom of the mountain. He was going to invite several of his friends, and Robin would bring some of her nursing buddies. "We will have so much fun," Robin said. "And Will is so handsome. My new mountain man."

The group had a great time dancing to a five-piece country band and sharing a picture of beer. The dance

THE SYSTEM • 99

club also had a small restaurant that served pizza and burgers. Will and Robin exchanged numbers and soon became great friends. Will came to Maverick several months later, for the July 4 holiday, and enjoyed a cookout and picnic with Sam, Angel, Laurel, and Mia. He adored both girls, and they formed an immediate bond with him.

Ten months later, Robin and Will were married in a small garden ceremony with Angel as matron of honor and Sam as best man. Laurel and Mia were the official flower girls. Robin's and Will's moms came to Florida for the wedding. It was a very special ceremony filled with love. "I am so very happy," Robin told her mom. "I never thought I would love again, but look at me now."

Robin and Will spent a lot of time with Laurel and Mia. The girls called him Papa, and he loved it. They took them on several great trips to the beaches, on a cruise, and to the Bahamas for a week on Paradise Island. On Robin and Will's first anniversary, Laurel announced that she wanted to go on anniversary too. So of course Papa caved, and they all went down the coast on "anniversary." Every time they stopped to eat, Laurel announced, "We are on anniversary," much to the amusement of the waitstaff and any nearby customers. She would be rewarded with a cupcake or an ice cream with sparkles and sometimes a lighted candle.

"We knew this day would eventually come, Mama," Sam said. He and Angel had received a notice from the court of another pending court date. Jill was again requesting unsupervised visitations for Joe with Laurel and Mia. Eight years had passed, and Joe was off house arrest, and his ankle-tracking device was removed. He was a free man. Laurel was nine years old; Mia was almost eight. Both children were beautiful and had outgoing, delightful personalities. They would be the perfect targets for Joe with his previous perverted behavior and pathology.

"I will finally get my way," Jill told Joe. "It will be so great to be able to have you and all three girls together at last." Joe agreed with anticipated thoughts running through his mind.

The court date was set for eight weeks, and they were the first case on the docket. Sam immediately contacted the DCF and the Partners for Strong Families to seek their advice about and support for blocking this petition. Both departments advised Sam that since Joe had served his time and completed his obligation to society, they could not recommend further supervised visitations, especially if the children were with their biological mother. They further advised that unless the children were actually hurt, their hands were tied. "Are you telling me that we have to wait until my children are molested before you will help us?" Sampson yelled. "This is totally unacceptable!"

Mr. Vu was again retained to represent Sam, Laurel, and Mia. Mr. Vu was not confident that the judge could legally block Jill's petition now that Joe was free and without recommendations for caution from the DCF or the Partners for Strong Families. Things looked very bleak.

In the meantime, Robin and Papa were discussing a drastic plan for intervention if the courts ruled in favor of Jill and Joe. As a former marine, Papa could not allow his precious granddaughters to be hurt by such evilness. "This will not happen," he promised Robin. He and Robin began their own surveillance on the couple. It was easy to determine the daily routines of Jill and Joe. They wrote down Jill's schedule at the Department of Corrections, where she still worked as a guard at the jail. They followed Joe as he left the trailer to take his daughter to school and then go to work. Their routines were very predictable. Robin and Papa's plan was made; now it was up to the courts. If the courts gave unsupervised visitation to Jill and Joe, they would have their final celebration on this earth.

It was all up to God. Robin and Papa got down on their knees, held hands, and cried out to God, "Lord, we have spent our lives serving your people in nursing and in combat for our country. Now look at what we are planning! Lord God, please stop this whole thing. Please wrap your loving and protective arms around these children and our family. Stop this, Jesus, we are begging you. We trust you, Lord, Your will be done." Robin and Papa prayed threw-out the night.

Mr. Vu discovered that only one month ago, Joe's ex-wife sued him for about $5,000 in back child support with the help of the Association Against Deadbeat Dads. Joe was served with a subpoena to go to court and the demand for full payment, or he would face real jail time. Jill took out a loan for the money and paid the owed child support so that her husband would not have to go to jail.

Mr. Vu further discovered that Jill had never paid a penny of her court-ordered child support of $200 per month for the past ten years. That meant a total of $24,000 was owed to Sam. With Sam's approval, Mr. Vu contacted both the Association Against Deadbeat Dads and Jill's attorney, advising the same action would be taken against Jill when she stepped into the county courthouse. Jill would have to make a down payment of another $5,000 via a cashier's check made out to Sampson or face her own jail time. Jill knew that a prison guard married to a man with Joe's reputation would not do well in this rural jailhouse. She did not have this kind of money and could not take out another loan. What was she to do? "I can't help you. My credit is bad, and I am broke. You and the baby take all my money. This is your problem. Count me out," Joe told her.

"Sam, you have no right to do this to me," Jill cried over the phone. "What more do you want from me? How can I stop this? You can't put me in jail."

Sam's reply was well thought out by having several consultations with Mr. Vu and the representative from the Association for Deadbeat Dads. " We'll work it out," he answered. Sam, Angel, and Robin discussed and prayed about the deal Mr. Vu would present to Jill and her attorney. The deal had two options. The first option was for Jill to present Sam with a $5,000 cashier's check at the courthouse and then agree to have her paycheck garnished monthly for the regular child support payment of $200 per month and an additional make-up payment of $200 per month for the next ten years until the back child support was paid and the children reached age eighteen. A total of $400 per month, without interest, would automatically come out of Jill's check, go through the courts, and be paid to Sam. The second option was very simple, and no one thought that it would be accepted. Jill would have to relinquish all parental rights to Laurel and Mia. They would remain in Sam's custody, and Jill would have no contact with them until they turned eighteen years old. Her name would be taken off their birth certificates, and Angel would be allowed to legally adopt Laurel and Mia with her name as mother. It would be as if Jill never existed. Jill's attorney strongly advised against this move, but Jill saw it as an easy way out. After all, she barely saw the girls. She had her other daughter and still had her husband, the love of her life. She accepted the second offer immediately. "Draw up the papers. Let's get this over with," she instructed her attorney. "I will have time later to explain my side of the story to Laurel and Mia. The name on the birth certificates doesn't mean anything anyway. They will know the truth and who I am. Let Sam and Angel have the hassle and expense of raising two girls. I will raise my own daughter."

The papers were drawn up, once more against the advice of Jill's attorney. They were signed by Jill and Sampson, approved by a ruling from the judge, and recorded by the clerk of the court. Prior to signing the papers Jill made one more demand. "I want to meet alone with Laurel and Mia and have them tell me that they don't want to see me anymore."

Sam's first response to this request was to deny it. "Why would you want to do that to the girls? Don't you think they have been through enough?" Sam finally allowed a last visit at a nearby restaurant, but he accompanied his children.

"I will see you both again in a few years if this is what you really want," Jill said. Tears in their eyes, Laurel and Mia shook their heads. They could not possibly understand what this meant as Sam, Robin, and Angel shielded them from these evil and tragic series of events over the past ten years. He took them back to the car and to Angel.

Just that fast, a ten-year battle with the system and the evil was over. The Lord heard the cries of Robin and Papa and intervened with one wave of his mighty hand. The many prayers for strength, wisdom, financial support, and safety were met in an orderly manner. The final plea to stop this horrible ordeal was made by the family, each person asking specifically for Joe to be denied access to Laurel and Mia. Jesus, in His perfect time frame, heard and answered everyone's prayers. The lessons learned by this family were seen in retrospect as the immediate needs of each traumatic situation took precedence in the minds and actions of each family member with the main goal of providing proactive protection to Laurel and Mia. Jesus answered each petition from Sam, Angel, Robin, and Papa.

The whole family met after everything was finalized at their favorite mom-and-pop restaurant. "The Lord does indeed work in mysterious ways, and His time line is definitely not our time line. But we are so happy and grateful for His resolution to this horrible experience, and we are so thankful that our girls were protected," said Sam. "I can't believe that this is finally over. I didn't think this would ever happen."

"It's been a long ten years, that's for sure," Robin exclaimed.

Angel beamed. "We can finally be a real family. No more worry and stress. Oh, Sam, I can adopt the girls! They can be my babies now." Sam chuckled at Angel's giddiness. There was a hint of sadness in his eyes as he thought about how happy Angel was to have his girls when their own mother had just signed them off. It baffled him, but thank God for this woman! She was a real blessing directly from heaven.

"We'll work on that adoption very soon. I promise," Sam said, hugging Angel tightly.

Robin and Papa just looked at each other silently, each thanking Jesus that he intervened before they had to implement their heinous plan. Would He forgive them? Could they have actually gone through with it?

Laurel and Mia, oblivious to what the adults were talking about, dove into their chicken fingers and fries. God is so good!

The scene was very different at the Harvy house. They rode home in Joe's truck, side by side, but did not speak a word. Jill was lost in her thoughts, and Joe becoming more and more enraged as he drove. They proceeded home, but did not pick up their daughter from the babysitter. They needed to talk, to make a new plan. When they got into the house, they began to argue. "I can't believe that stupid judge did not give us unsupervised visitations," Jill said. "My lawyer assured me that the courts and DCF would favor me as their real mother. Well, we won't have to worry about having to pay for Laurel and Mia for another eight or nine years. We have our own family." she smirked.

Joe was furious with her. He had waited so long to become Laurel and Mia's stepdaddy. They were so pretty now, and just the right age for him. He had fantasized about them for two years now, and this stupid woman just signed them off. "How could you have done this idiotic thing without consulting me first? How could you just sell your own kids?" he screamed at her. "I had plans for them. I wanted to be their daddy and love and play with them. I hate you so much right now!" With that, Joe slapped her across the face, hard.

Jill looked at him in complete surprise. She had never been hit before; even as a correction's officer, no one had hit her. Her face hurt, and her eye began to swell. Joe, encouraged by how good that felt, doubled up his fist and slammed it into her belly. As she doubled over in pain, he hit her in the jaw with an uppercut, and she fell to the floor, completely knocked out. "Stupid woman, you have ruined everything," he said to her limp form. Joe had to get out of there before she came to. He grabbed several black trash bags out of the kitchen and threw his clothes, shoes, and bathroom necessities into them. After taking a last look around, he left Jill lying on the floor and drove off in his truck.

Jill came to about an hour later. She couldn't believe that Joe would hurt her, but seeing the blood on the floor from her split lips, seeing her eye swollen shut and purple, and feeling the pain in her stomach and jaw, she knew that she had pushed him too far. *He'll come back. He loves me. He told me so many times. I know he will come back,* she thought. She did not call the police or press charges.

EPILOGUE

S am and Angel just celebrated their thirty-fifth anniversary. They had a son, who is now in college in the health-care field. They are very active in their children's lives and have their grandchildren almost every weekend.

Laurel is a schoolteacher and has a handsome, hardworking husband and three wonderful children. She is active in her local church, helps with vacation Bible school during the summer, and coaches a girls' sports team at her school.

Mia has a degree in agriculture and is active in the county environmental control department. She is married to a rancher who raises beefalo, which are a buffalo/black Angus crossbreed that provides lean but flavorful meat to be sold around the country. They have a beautiful daughter and two sons.

Robin and Papa are living the good life and enjoying their grandchildren and great-grandchildren. Robin had a very difficult time forgiving Jill, Pete, Lisa Mae, and Joe. She spoke the words but had to confess that her heart was hardened. Several years ago, the Holy Spirit convicted her of this sin, and she finally found it in her heart to honestly forgive these people. Although it is difficult, Robin continues to pray for their souls.

Jill divorced Joe after he beat her up. She did not press charges and moved out of Florida. A few months later, she married a man who was twenty-one years older than her and resembled her father. Jill made several unsuccessful attempts to talk to Laurel and Mia and tell them her side of the story. They could see her pathology but also that she was indeed victimized by her parents and society. Although they felt sorry for her, neither wanted her around their children. Joe left the area and has not resurfaced. It will be God's job to judge.

The system has not changed in the past twenty years. Although it means well and employs many dedicated people, it is restricted to being reactive rather than proactive. Many children suffer at the hands of abusers—sexual, emotional, and physical—when they do not have a champion to keep them safe. It is in the hands of the champions to provide proactive protection to our children, to defy the system, and to bring God back into our lives.

GOD'S GRACE

"Let us therefore come boldly unto the
throne of grace, that we may obtain mercy
and find grace to help in time of need."
— *Hebrews 4:16 KJV*

ORGANIZATIONS DEDICATED TO CHILD SAFETY/PROTECTION

NATIONAL

National Child Abuse Hotline: 1-800-4ACHILD (800-422-4453)

https://www.nationalchildsafetycouncil.org

A Law Enforcement Partner Since 1955. NCSC is the oldest and largest 501(c)(3) federal tax-exempt, not-for-profit charitable organization dedicated to the safety of children. The Council leads the industry, by providing thousands of public safety organizations across the U.S. nearly 4.2 million pieces of safety material annually.

https://www.pfsf.org

Partnership for Strong Families provides child welfare services designed to protect local children from abuse, neglect and abandonment and assists in establishing safe and permanent homes with their own families, partner families or adoptive parents.

https://www.usa.gov/federal-agencies/administra tion-for-children-and-families

The Administration for Children and Families funds state, territory, local, and tribal organizations to provide family assistance (welfare), child support, child care, Head Start, child welfare, and other programs relating to children and families.

https://www.nationalcac.org

The National Children's Advocacy Center is a non-profit organization that provides training, prevention, and treatment services to fight child abuse and neglect.

https://oig.hhs.gov/fraud/child-support-enforcement

Office of Inspector General's (OIG) mission is to protect the integrity of Department of Health & Human Services (HHS) programs as well as the health and welfare of program beneficiaries. Parents who fail to pay court-ordered support for the care of their children put an unnecessary strain on the custodial parent and the children, as well as on agencies that are tasked with enforcing these matters. Although most child support cases fall under State and local jurisdiction, the Office of Inspector General (OIG) plays an important role in investigating particular cases regarding parents who fail to pay court-ordered child support.

To report suspected cases of fraud, waste, or abuse in Federal HHS programs, use our online OIG Hotline form. You may also call or fax us using the information below.

Phone: (800) HHS-TIPS [(800) 447-8477
Fax: (800) 223-8164
TTY: (800) 377-4950

https://www.avvo.com/child-abuse-lawyer.html
If a child has been the victim of emotional, physical, or sexual abuse, a child abuse lawyer can help you figure out the right child custody, visitation, or guardianship to protect the child.

FLORIDA

Abuse Hotline 1-800-962-2873, Florida Relay 711 or TTY: 1-800-955-8771

https://www.myflfamilies.com

The Florida Department of Children Families is committed to its mission of protecting the vulnerable, promoting strong and economically self-sufficient families, and advancing personal and family recovery and resiliency.

www.floridahealth.gov

Division of Children's Medical Services (CMS) is a collection of programs that serve children with special health care needs. Each program provides family-centered care using statewide networks of specially qualified doctors, nurses, and other healthcare professionals.

www.cms-kids.com.

The Division of Children's Medical Services will provide information about CMS programs pertaining to Child Protection.

https://www.supportcollectors.com/resources/florida-laws-and-resources

The Florida Child Support Enforcement is the state-run child support enforcement office for Florida. The Florida Department of Revenue is required by federal law to provide services through Child Support Enforcement (CSE) and is funded by the federal government and the State of Florida.

If you would like to discuss your case in further detail with an advisor at our child support agency, we can be reached Monday through Friday toll-free at: 1-888-729-6661 between 8:00 a.m. and 7:00 p.m. (CST).

Lightning Source UK Ltd.
Milton Keynes UK
UKHW010706240520
363742UK00004B/127/J